RAPT

An Erotic Tale

LAUREL CREMANT

RAPT
An Erotic Tale
By Laurel Cremant

Copyright © 2014 by Laurel Cremant

ISBN: 978-0-9916357-0-2

Cover Design by James, GoOnWrite.com

Print Edition

Winged Moon Publishing, LLC
Hollywood, Florida

This is a work of fiction. Names, characters, places and incidents either are the product of the author's imagination or are used fictitiously, and any resemblance to actual persons living or dead, business establishments, events or locales, is entirely confidential.

Jessica Sinclair has spent the last year tip toeing around her new boss Lucas Wright. She wants him and he knows it, but she has no intention of giving into temptation. She's always enjoyed a little pain with her pleasure, but she never thought denial could feel so good. Every meeting drives her to a sexual edge and yet they've never shared a simple kiss. Resisting him has become a delicious game.

Lucas Wright has enjoyed playing the waiting game with Jessica. The sadist in him enjoys every quip and parry they share. But every man has his limits and he's officially reached his. He'd never thought that he would find his perfect match in a woman as stubborn as Jessica, but every teasing encounter has convinced him it's time to put an end to their games and show her just how sweet surrender can be.

For all the readers who like it hot and for the readers who love it spicy…This one is for you.

One

"Will you walk into my parlour?" said the spider to the fly.

LUCAS WRIGHT SMILED as he thought of the line from an old children's fable. He'd never considered himself a predator, but the ever-pressing need to devour one Ms. Jessica Wright convinced him otherwise. For almost a year, he had wanted nothing more than to drag her to his bed and wrap her in so much pleasure she'd never leave.

He shook his head derisively as he stood up from his workout mat. Sweat dripped down his bare chest and abdomen. Even after almost two exhausting hours of intense yoga, his muscles tightened and his cock stirred to attention at the image of her forming in his mind, all bothered and wet, stretched out on his bed.

Soon.

Today, he planned to take action.

He walked to edge of his hotel suite and stepped out onto the large glass rimmed balcony. Pulling in a deep breath, he let the warm salty breeze of the Fort Lauderdale coastline fill his lungs and calm his building anticipation. By tonight, he would know for sure whether Jessica was willing to take their flirtations to another level.

If she's honest with herself.

And that was the crux of it. He wondered if she was ready to admit that they'd both been playing a long drawn out game for quite some time. Each of them pushing the boundaries of their professional relationship and testing the waters. For months, they had danced around each other, whether Jessica chose to admit it or not. In the beginning, he'd almost missed it. Caught up in his own need to control his attraction and baser instincts he'd almost missed the signs.

Lucas hired her to be his chief acquisitions actuary. His company specialized in mergers and acquisitions. When his previous actuary retired, Jessica had come highly recommended. Upon reviewing her resume, he noted she was bright, driven, and after interviewing her for over an hour, he'd added tenacious and perfect for the job to her list of qualifications.

However, from the moment Jessica stepped into his office he'd wanted her for more than just her skills in the field. She'd reminded him of a painting he purchased several years before. Titled Calypso, the picture depicted a curvaceous, naked black woman sprawled on a throne, her head turned as she stared out at the ocean. One leg dangled over the side of the chair while the other trailed on the floor, her feet pointed and delicate looking. The painting had hit him like a punch to the gut and he'd purchased it on the spot. The first time he met Jessica he had the same reaction.

He'd been instantly attracted by the soft lush curves hugged underneath her deep gray pencil skirt. The full pout of her full lips as she spoke to him in a soft husky voice had him aroused in seconds and the creamy smoothness of her chocolate skin had him itching to reach out and test its softness. Every inch of her seemed designed to entice him—from her warm brown eyes, down her luscious body, to the point of her stiletto-heeled shoes. She exuded a combination of confidence and intelligence that only added to her allure. However, at the age of thirty-eight, he'd learned enough in his lifetime to not to let attraction get in the way of business.

He had a hard and staunch rule of never mixing business with pleasure. Aside from it just being a sound business practice, his rule allowed him to maintain a certain level of privacy. One of the pitfalls of owning a company as large as his was that people became inordinately interested in his personal life. Since he had no intention of handing over his business or going broke anytime soon—it was drawback to success he accepted whole-heartedly.

His sexual preferences were also a part of his need for privacy. Although he didn't fully immerse himself into the world of BDSM, he'd learned a long time ago that he was a moderate sexual sadist. Unlike most people, his revelation didn't come as an epiphany or gradual understanding of his psyche. Growing up with two college professors as parents he was surrounded by scientific and medical journals his entire life. By the time he had his first sexual experience, he'd recognized and accepted his sexuality. He'd even had a few rather frank discussions with his parents regarding the matter. Being the child of two very progressive, former hippie parents had its advantages.

However, embracing his sexuality didn't mean he wanted it open to public discussion. He was very selective in choosing lovers. Although he didn't find it difficult to find women willing to dabble in his lifestyle, over the last few years he wanted more and more a woman willing to play long-term.

The clock is ticking.

He smiled derisively at that thought. Lately he'd felt as if time was ticking by too quickly. He'd grown up an only child and had always wanted a large family. Although he wanted a woman willing to submit her pleasure to him in bed, he also wanted a strong female role model for his future children. He looked back on the long drawn out discussions his parents would have at the dinner table with fondness. They discussed everything from movies to global geopolitics with passion and he wanted that same type of relationship with the woman he chose to marry. Finding that woman seemed easier said than done—until he'd met Jessica.

Jessica had surprised him. Not only did he find the tall, dark beauty sexy, he appreciated her keen intelligence and sharp wit. Every now and then he would sense vulnerability in her, but her take charge, no-nonsense personality masked any softness well. That combination of hard and soft intrigued him and had the sadist and him, among other things, standing at attention.

She personified the type of woman he wanted to pursue and so much more. It took him a while to admit that he'd fallen for her but something about her tugged at him, making it difficult for him to ignore. His stance of not mixing business with pleasure had been the only thing holding him back. However, all that changed when he realized, Jessica was fighting the same attraction. Not only that—she also seemed to enjoy the mounting sexual tension as much as he did. It seemed his sexy actuary exhibited a touch of sexual masochism.

It started small. He'd notice her long glances down his body when she thought no one was looking, her hitched breathing as their meetings progressed—the hard pebbling of her nipples beneath her blouse. He'd recognized those signs.

When he first began exploring the BDSM lifestyle, he'd encountered more than a few masochists who enjoyed prolonging sexual stimulation. One woman in particular enjoyed masturbating for days prior to seeking any relief. He could see her glassy eyed arousal mirrored in Jessica's behavior as the months progressed.

He began anticipating each meeting with her. Testing her limits by prolonging their discussions and watching her body tighten and squirm with each passing minute. The air hung heavy with the scent of her arousal—the ultimate aphrodisiac. He'd inhaled the scent his mouth watering at the implication. He marveled that she thought he wouldn't notice how aroused she was as she sat in front of him, crossing and uncrossing her legs every few minutes. He dragged that meeting out—the sadist in him couldn't help it—and watched as her breath caught repeatedly.

When he finally decided to end the meeting, she stood on shaky legs as he escorted her out of the office. Even after tormenting her for so long he couldn't resist the urge to confirm his suspicions. As he'd reached to open the door, he deliberately grazed his arm against the front of her blouse, sweeping across her hard nipples. Her slick lips fell open on a gasp, and her eyes had blazed with an almost crazed passion.

He let her escape that day with a murmured apology, he'd watched her stumble down the hall to her office and slam the door shut—his lips curling up in a wide grin.

There was nothing a sadist liked better than a game of denial and patience.

He'd been playing the same game ever since. Knowing she was aroused, prolonging meetings to see just how long she could last. Their meetings were becoming an addiction for him and fantasizing about what she did each time she left him kept his body on overdrive and caused more than a few sleepless nights.

Not many women were into his preferred method of sexual dominance. His brand of sadism focused almost exclusively on sexual denial—on having a woman submit control to him and allowing him to decide when they would receive pleasure. The slow delay or denial of pleasure and gradual buildup of arousal gave him the power to deconstruct a person's orgasm. That type of power dynamic and play turned him on like nothing else. Finding a partner to indulge with proved more difficult than most people would think.

Most women loved the concept of extended foreplay, but when he prolonged it passed an hour or more without allowing them to come, they weren't exactly happy to meet his acquaintance.

Leaning his elbows on the railing, he stared out over the small crowd of sunbathers and tourists below on the beach, his gaze resting the perfect cerulean blue of the ocean beyond.

Lucas recalled the brief emails she'd exchanged with him that day and released a short breath. Her current assignment was over and as usual, she would make her way to him to deliver her final report and analysis in person. In a little over an hour Jessica would arrive and the anticipation of it was already tightening his skin and heating his blood. To tell the truth he'd been running on high since the moment she'd messaged him earlier in the day. He'd prolonged his yoga routine in the hopes of exhausting his body and diminishing his libido.

No such luck.

He should have known better. Pushing back from the rail, he turned and walked back into his suite and stretched his arms over head, trying to release the mounting tension spreading across his shoulders. Dropping his hands down to his waist he untied his drawstring pants and let them fall to the floor before making his way into the bathroom. He stepped into the cool marble shower enclosure and locked his knees tight before twisting on the water.

He whispered a soft curse as cold water sluiced down his body. As the freezing water beat down on his skin, Lucas consoled himself with a single thought. Tonight he would either find relief or learn definitively that Jessica was hands off.

***

The office smelled like sex—again.

Jessica Wright cut her gaze to the flustered woman holding the door open for her. The woman's lips were swollen and bare of lipstick while her high cheekbones were tinged a bright hue of red. All of that, combined with the woman's mussed hair and rumpled clothing, left Jessica with no doubt that the woman and the man sitting smugly at his desk had just engaged in some extracurricular office activity.

I don't get paid enough for this.

Releasing her breath in a quick huff, Jessica stepped over the threshold into the sleek office of Shepard Electronics CEO, Richard Planks. The door closed with a soft snick behind her. Despite her disgust for Planks, she couldn't keep her pulse from speeding up in anticipation. Not for her meeting with Planks but for what would happen afterward. Dealing with Planks now meant she would see Lucas Wright later.

Lucas Wright. Her current employer and guilty pleasure. Because of him her usual enjoyment of dealing with scum like Planks was heightened with the knowledge that seeing Wright always followed. Tingling pinpricks raced across her skin and her palms began to sweat. Suppressing the need to rub them down the sides of her skirt she kept her gaze trained on Planks.

"I hope I didn't interrupt anything important," she said as she walked towards him.

"Nothing that couldn't be rescheduled," he replied in the low nasal drawl indicative of his Bostonian roots.

Oh, I'm sure.

He didn't rise from his seat as she entered the room. Not that she expected him to. The man was sleazy arrogance personified. He'd made it clear since she first arrived several weeks ago, that he wasn't worried about what her investigation might find. That didn't surprise her. In her line of work she'd found that regardless of level of wealth—greed and hubris were equal opportunity vices amongst people in powerful positions.

Richard Planks indulged in both to the point of addiction.

He sat at his desk, his tailored suite rumpled, a satisfied smile twitching at his lips. She wondered for the hundredth time, how a man so stupid managed to become CEO of such a large corporation. She'd perused thousands of financial data proving her assessment. Richard Planks wasn't only a sleaze—he was also a thief and a cheat. And the man truly believed his machinations wouldn't be discovered.

Fool.

She didn't wait for permission to be seated. Planks wasn't the type to extend an invitation. He liked people to feel uncomfortable around him. Jessica had no patience for his silly power play. Sitting down, she leaned back into the soft leather chair and crossed her legs. She watched as his gaze followed the movement of her legs, lingering for a moment on the small stretch of thigh revealed by the hem of her skirt. The leer curling across his features didn't bother her. It only served to make the moment to come so much sweeter.

Her lips trembled as she tried to keep a wide smile from stretching across her mouth. This was the part of her job she loved the most—the moment when smug men like Planks were gob-smacked with truth.

She'd spent years studying and training to become an actuary and for the last year she'd had the exclusive pleasure of being Lucas Wright's acquisitions actuary. Her main job function was to investigate the viability of companies like Shepard Electronics and determine whether they were worth Wright's time and money to acquire. Most people assumed that the world of mergers and acquisitions was all about hostile takeovers, but a good portion of the deals were mutual and in Planks case much welcomed.

Obviously, he couldn't wait to shake himself of his burgeoning electronic firm. His eagerness wouldn't normally be a red flag. Some people were honest enough with themselves to know when they'd taken their companies as far as their abilities and assets allowed. Yet from their first meeting Jessica knew Planks was far from humble. No— his eagerness to be acquired by Wright Inc. had little to do with humility and everything to do with greed and like most men of his ilk, he assumed that no one would figure out his schemes.

"I hope you've found everything you need."

He said the words in dismissive nonchalance fueling her excitement.

She smoothed her thumb along the file folder in her hand. It contained a copy of her final report, detailing the viability of Planks' company and whether or not it represented a good investment.

This is going to be fun.

"Yes. Actually, I was able to complete my final analysis this afternoon. I sent it over to Mr. Wright before coming to see you," she said.

"Wonderful. I'll let my lawyers know to begin the paperwork so that we can move forward."

"That won't be necessary." She leaned forward and placed the file on the desk.

"Mr. Wright has elected to withdraw his bid for Shepard Electronics."

She watched as her words penetrated the thick fog of arrogance surrounding him. It didn't take long. His eyes widened for a brief moment before narrowing in anger while his smirking lips firmed into a grim line.

"What the hell are you talking about?"

He jacked forward in his chair and snatched the file open. His gaze blazing across the lines she'd enjoyed typing with relish.

Satisfaction skittered through her. Yes—moments like these were exactly why she loved her job. Some children grew up wanting to be doctors, firefighters or astronauts. She'd grown up wanting to make men like Planks wallow in their own failure.

A therapist might say her satisfaction stemmed from a childhood filled with disappointments caused by inattentive socialite parents, along with a dose of resentment at being abandoned. After authorities discovered their lavish lifestyle had been funded by a myriad of embezzlement and

Ponzi schemes her parents fled the country in fear of imprisonment. Had they repented in any way? No. They merely chose a country with no extradition agreements with the United States and continued to live without care for their actions or daughter. Since Jessica was well aware of her motivations and baggage, she had no problem with forgoing potentially massive therapy bills for the lucrative six-figure salary she received by taking men like Planks down instead.

"I found the transfers. It took me a little while, but the thing about money is that it always leaves a trail. No business is squeaky clean, but those hefty deposits you've been moving into your accounts…"

She shook her head and pursed her lips—letting out a short tsking sound.

"Not a very smart move. So I'm sure you can understand why Mr. Wright wouldn't want to move forward with a company whose profit margins have been faked for the last six quarters," she said.

The crunching sound of paper rent the air as his fist clenched around the file. His knuckles paled into a glowing white; a stark contrast to the deep red flush racing up his neck to cover his scowling face in an angry mask.

"You fucking bitch!"

She raised an eyebrow at his snarled accusation.

Typical.

It never ceased to amaze her how easy some people found it necessary to resort to name-calling. On some level, she appreciated the last attempt at a jab. After all, in Planks' case she had just guaranteed that his family and colleagues would learn of his dirty dealings.

"Thank you," she said as she rose from her seat.

He leapt to his feet and leaned forward—bracing his hands down on the desk.

"You can't do this!"

Her gaze flicked down his body briefly before meeting his eyes dead on.

"I just did."

She turned on her heel and walked to the door—a string of expletives and curses raining down her back as she reached for the knob. She paused for a moment there.

"By the way. You might want to wipe the lipstick stains from your slacks before you go meet with your board of directors."

With that, she strode from the office, her only thoughts focused on seeing Lucas again.

Two

JESSICA DIDN'T LOOK back as she made her way down the long hall to the elevator bank. As far as she was concerned, Richard Planks and his failing company were already old news. She pressed the call button and fought the urge to tap her foot in impatience. The quicker she left the building, the sooner she could see Lucas.

The slight buzz of her phone set off an answering shiver through her body. Her nipples tightened in awareness and a small flare of heat settled in her stomach.

Lucas.

Without looking, she knew it would be him. Reaching into the side pocket of her purse, she retrieved her phone, her fingers trembled as she accepted the call.

"Is it done?"

His husky voice washed over her and she locked her knees against the urge to sway to it.

"Yes."

"Good. There's a car waiting downstairs. I'll see you soon."

He didn't wait for a reply. He didn't need to, Jessica didn't intend to miss their meeting—she never did.

The elevator dinged to a stop and she stepped inside already wondering where she would meet Lucas this time. Although, his company headquartered in Chicago, Lucas spent a good amount of his weeks traveling, but he always insisted on being briefed in person. Most times, she met him in a nearby city to discuss her final analysis. It was usually just a formality, one she looked forward to.

He had offices in multiple states. Depending on his location at any given moment, their meetings took place wherever he chose. Sometimes they would meet at a restaurant, sometimes at whatever hotel or home he was renting for the moment. Those were the most thrilling for her—the ones that tested her control the most. Sitting in a hotel suite, knowing that a large soft bed would be only a door away, always took her to the edge of control.

The elevator came to a stop and the doors opened with a smooth swishing sound shaking her from her thoughts. She smoothed a sweaty palm down the side of her skirt and stepped out into the lobby. With quick strides, she made her way through the mid-afternoon throng of business people and walked out into the balmy downtown Miami air.

"Ms. Sinclair."

Standing just at the edge of the sidewalk beside a black stretch limousine was Lucas' driver and all around fix-it-man, Eli. Wherever Lucas went, Eli wasn't too far behind. She suspected that he was more than just a driver and sometimes assistant. With his tall, buff body and constantly scanning eyes, she wouldn't be surprised to learn that part of his duties involved security and body-guarding. Jessica shook her head at him as she approached.

"How many times do I have to tell you to call me Jessica?"

"I don't know, but I'll tell you when I do."

He opened the door to the limo and gestured her inside.

"Cute," she said smiling as she slid into the car.

"I think so," he said before closing the door.

Laughing softly to herself, she settled back into the plush leather seat and let out a sigh. Closing her eyes, she pictured Lucas in her mind. She didn't have to wonder about what he would be wearing, in that aspect he was always predictable. Dark tailored suits were his outfits of choice. Considering he ran such a high profile business, that didn't surprise her.

Nothing about Lucas Wright disappointed. From his pale skin contrasting against his curling shock of dark red hair and golden-hazel eyes, to the hard square cut of his jaw, or the sensuous curve of his thick lips, Lucas was built to impress. His tall frame was wide and thick, reminding her of pictures she'd seen of burly lumberjacks and Mounties. He'd mentioned once that he enjoyed practicing power yoga and it showed. His longs legs were topped with large, hard thighs and a tight muscled ass. How he managed to stuff all of that muscle and bone into a business suit, every morning amazed her. Nevertheless, she was grateful for it. The tailored lines encased his body to perfection, making her want to peel him out of them, one strip of fabric at a time.

As the car swung into traffic, her fingers itched to press the call button. It would only take a quick question to Eli to learn where they were headed. Instead, she clenched her fingers tight. Not knowing was half the fun.

Until she'd met Lucas, she'd never fully accepted how much she craved denial. It was a strange realization to learn at her age. Her thirty-third birthday was only a few months away and yet it wasn't until recently that she'd admitted certain things to herself. Since her first experience with sex, she'd known foreplay was an experience she couldn't forgo. Quickies were fine and they had their place, but teasing, anticipation and denial were her favorite indulgences. She'd thought that was normal. After all, television talk shows and magazine covers like *Glamour*, *Vogue*, and *Cosmo* touted tips for prolonging foreplay all the time.

The first time she had a lover complain about her want for prolonged foreplay, she chalked it up to his impatience. In the end, she usually reached orgasm, but only with an extended effort from her partner. As she got more engrossed in her career, finding time to date required too much effort. Every now and then, she would indulge in a short affair or one nightstand. Those encounters never really left her fully satisfied but she appreciated the sexual release. No matter how tame it would be. However, once she met Lucas, her entire outlook changed.

Pulling a hand through her long curling hair, she recalled the instant tingling sensation she had when she first met the eccentric executive. Something about him had her libido at attention from the very start. It was a new experience for her—that instant jolt of lust—but she'd tamped it down. She didn't believe in engaging in affairs at work, especially not with her boss. She'd seen more than one career ruined by that type of power dynamic. However, with each meeting, with each conversation, she found herself more and more drawn to him, and as the year wore on, it had become a kind of game for her.

She fantasized about him constantly. At night, she would think of him as she touched herself, imagining his large hands rubbing up and down her body, his shaft stroking in and out of her. His hot husky voice would whisper dirty things in her ear. She teased herself like that for long moments sometimes hours, but never allowed herself to come. That she saved for their meetings—specifically for the nights she lay in bed alone *after* their meetings. Seeing him was always her endgame—the catalyst she allowed herself to climax. It was a naughty game she liked to play, but it was one that taught her a lot about herself, her desires and her needs.

Working with Lucas had changed her irrevocably. She could never go back to her old acceptance of 'normal sex' again.

Sighing, she stared out the window noting the fast cars whizzing by. They were driving on the expressway heading north.

Fort Lauderdale maybe?

She shrugged her shoulders. It didn't matter where they were heading, all that mattered was that tonight she'd find some relief from the strain she put on her body. Her skin felt painfully tight—small trickles of sweat beaded between her breasts and her panties were damp with arousal. Crossing her legs, she bit back a whimper at the friction it caused on her clit.

This assignment had lasted longer than usual, testing her limits. Yet even when she'd realized this, she didn't refrain from masturbating every night. Each night she played with herself, taking herself to an almost unbearable edge before stopping, denying herself the relief of climax. She knew she was playing with fire but couldn't resist. The releases she eventually obtained were like a drug.

Her games had almost backfired once before, when a scheduled meeting with Lucas was postponed for two weeks. She hadn't stopped her ritual of tease and denial, so by the time she'd finally met with him she was ready to burst. That marked the first and only time, she didn't wait to get home until she relieved herself.

She squirmed in her seat. Thinking of that day skyrocketed her temperature even higher. She pulled out her phone and glanced at the time. They'd been on the road almost twenty minutes. Giving into temptation, she pressed the small call button on the inside of her door.

"Eli, how much longer until we get there?"

"Not much longer. Barring any heavy traffic we should arrive in about ten minutes."

"Thank you."

She released the button and leaned back in her seat, sighing with a mixture of relief and disappointment—relief because Eli's reply helped bank some of her rising anxiety, and disappointment because with that relief came a slight drop in her arousal.

"Masochist."

She whispered the word with a reluctant smile.

Admitting the truth to herself had become somewhat easier in the last few months. It summed up her love of extended sexual denial perfectly. When she'd first realized how powerful her orgasms were after one of her long sessions of foreplay, she'd done some research and discovered a wealth of information in several on-line chat rooms. There, she learned that she wasn't an anomaly and had nothing to be ashamed of. However, she had been surprised to learn that sexual denial fell under the BDSM lifestyle.

The idea of having physical pain inflicted on herself, either through flogging or spanking or any of the various overwhelming ways she'd learned on those sites, didn't turn her on. The idea of having someone control and deny her pleasure did. Since her last assignment for Lucas, she'd even contemplated exploring a Dominant/submissive relationship, but the idea of submitting to anyone other than Lucas left her cold—a circumstance that continued to frustrate her.

To tell the truth, she didn't know much about him, but the few personal tidbits, she'd learned about him had kept her intrigued.

Lucas didn't fit her model of a corporate shark. He had confidence and arrogance in spades. Such qualities she expected and even respected in people who were willing to work hard towards a goal. Unlike her father, Lucas lived and breathed ambition. He had no qualms about working hard towards a goal and earning his money honestly. Unlike like other ambitious men she'd met, Lucas had an uncanny ability to relax. A skill that often amused and annoyed her in equal measure. Although he traveled a lot on business, he didn't believe in extended workdays. Barring any emergencies, he stopped working every day at precisely six-thirty in the evening. It was well known throughout the company that weekends were sacrosanct. The policies were great for employee morale, but murder on people like Jessica who liked all loose ends tied up neat and clean at the end of each day.

He smiled a lot as well—always quick to tell a joke or even prank an executive now and then. In many ways, he reminded her of over-aged playful frat boy.

And the tests.

She blew out a breath at the thought. Yes—the tests. Lucas' parents were both professors at Northwestern University. His father was an acclaimed psychologist and his mother a biochemist who'd conducted several famous experiments on health and mortality. With those two brilliant minds as parents, Jessica supposed Lucas' obsession with physical and mental well-being shouldn't be a surprise. However, his habit of declaring random paid mental health days wreaked havoc on her work schedule. In addition, he had a penchant for administering the strangest questionnaires and tests aimed at determining which employees worked best with each other and understanding everyone's work personality. As much as his ways puzzled her, she found him refreshing. He genuinely wanted everyone to have what he thought was a healthy work environment.

As a whole package, she found him intriguing and that made it harder and harder for her to separate her fantasy from the real man. Gradually she'd found herself wanting to learn more about him—to take more away from their encounters than the promise of sexual relief. She wanted to know more about what made him tick, what other goals he had in life outside of business, what else made him laugh... what made him aroused.

She let out a small snort at her thoughts.

Pathetic.

Only she would mess up a perfectly fine fantasy with emotional entanglement, but she wanted more. She had been contemplating approaching Lucas directly—of letting him know that she was interested in him.

Yeah right.

Interested didn't begin to cover her feelings for Lucas. The truth was, during the course of the year she'd fallen more than a little bit in love with the man. Somewhere between fantasy and reality, she'd let her heart get involved. She didn't know what to do and didn't trust her feelings. How much of them were tangled up in the man she created in her fantasies and how much in the actual man?

She smoothed her hand across her hair, checking to make sure no loose curls escaped her bun. It was a nervous habit—one she knew signaled her growing distress. Blowing out a breath, she dropped her hand back to her lap.

It wasn't as if she was hideous. She knew men found her attractive. Would it be so hard to approach Lucas?

Despite his professional demeanor, she had caught the occasional hot look he threw her way. However, the risk of disappointment held her back. Not only had he starred in all of her fantasies for the better part of a year, he had fulfilled her need for denial in a way she was unsure he could do in real life. How exactly did one go about telling their lover that they were a sexual masochist?

That simply asked question was difficult for her to answer. Although, she'd gradually grown to accept what she needed in a sexual relationship, she didn't think she could bear it if Lucas rejected her because of it. Choosing to ignore the problem for now, Jessica focused on re-igniting her arousal instead.

The car turned, merging off the highway into local traffic. Remembering Eli's estimate of time, she calculated she had a few minutes left to up the stakes.

Glancing at the darkened partition separating the back of the limo from the front driver's cabin, she reached underneath her skirt and pulled down her panties. Slipping the silky material down her legs, she stepped out of them and tucked them securely in her bag. Leaning back in her seat she spread her legs slightly and trailed her fingers up her inner thighs.

Muffling a whimper, she pulled an image of Lucas up in her head. She imagined him sitting across from her, watching her fingers inch closer and closer up to her pussy. Imagined him telling her to spread her legs wider—to show him how much she wanted him.

She held that image in her head, stroking her thighs but not slipping her fingers into her wet folds. That she would save for later—after she left Lucas and was alone again.

For now, she indulged herself in her fantasy. Long minutes passed before she reached a hand up and cupped her left breast over her silk pink blouse. She curved her hand around the sensitive globe, avoiding caressing her nipple—that too she would save for later. She enjoyed squeezing it and smoothing her thumb just below the areola.

The car began to slow and reluctantly she pulled her skirt back down to her knees and clasped her hands in her lap.

She looked out of the window again and saw the sophisticated emblem of a hotel flash by, just as Eli pulled the car into a curved parkway.

The Ritz-Carlton.

She clenched her thighs tight—her already heated body, blazing up a notch. Meeting with Lucas already had her hot, but the idea of being alone with him so close to a large bouncy bed, was almost more than she could take.

Taking in deep breaths, she struggled to bring her arousal back under control.

The door opened and Eli stood waiting with his hand outstretched to help her out of the car. Grateful for the assistance she placed her trembling fingers in his and allowed him to help her from the car.

"Mr. Wright is in the penthouse suite," he said.

She nodded her head as he escorted her through the hotel. They passed the main elevator bank before turning a corner. At the end of the hall was another door. Eli reached forward and typed in a short code on a small keypad next to the door. After a moment, the door slid open and Jessica realized it masked a private elevator. She stepped inside and turned just in time to see Eli give her a small, mock salute before he turned and walked away.

The door quickly shut, and in less than a minute slid open again onto a small light filled atrium.

Before she could look around the small foyer Lucas' handsome face filled her gaze.

"What took you so long?" he asked, his golden eyes twinkling down at her.

Whatever calm she had reached during the short walk through the lobby and her ride up to his suite quickly disappeared. She took a deep swallow as her gaze slid down his body. He stood with his arms crossed over his chest and legs planted slightly apart. Instead of his usual suit, dark colored worn jeans hugged his thick thighs and a simple white polo shirt stretched across his broad chest, straining against the bulky muscles of his upper arms.

"Follow me," he said before turning and marching through an adjacent doorway off to the side.

Her eyes rested on the smooth curves of his ass as it bunched and flexed while her strode away.

Biting her lips, she held back a whimper. This meeting would definitely test her limits and for the first time she wasn't sure if she could make it.

Three

LUCAS STRODE INTO the main living area of the suite trying his best to suppress a groan. His dick hardened the moment Jessica had stepped from the elevator. Her eyes blazed with arousal and it was all he could do to keep from pushing her up against the nearest wall and licking his way into that deliciously sexy mouth of hers. His mouth watered at that thought. He wondered if she would taste as decadent and as sinful as she looked.

He hesitated at the small sofa centered in the middle of the floor, but changed his mind and continued on to the large desk nestled in the corner of the room. Stepping behind it, he turned and sat down onto a sleek leather seat and watched her approach.

Watching Jessica enter any room always held his attention. Her hips undulated to some sultry unheard rhythm, but damn if he didn't want to learn the tune.

Before her, he considered himself a lover of all women in every shape and size, but now he couldn't imagine curling up at night against anything except her ample curves. She had the classic hourglass shape of and old-fashioned pin-up model and she always dressed to accentuate instead of hide it. He liked that about her. If anyone was ever foolish enough to mistake her femininity for weakness or lack of intelligence, it only took a few words from her quick tongue to set them straight.

Just thinking about the few times he'd seen her do just that kicked his pulse up a notch. Trying to corral his thoughts to the safer, less deviant parts of his mind, he focused his gaze back on her face.

"How did Planks take the news?" he asked without preamble.

"How do you think?" she replied as she paused in front of the desk.

She sat down in the lone chair facing him and placed her purse on the floor next to her feet. He watched her face as she crossed her long legs. A slight tremble worked her lips and he wondered whether she wore any underwear—a question he asked himself ever since he realized her secret. He had every confidence the answer was a definitive no.

"I'm sure he took it like the honest and amicable man he is," he said.

She snorted.

"Of course. Have you had a chance to read the rest of my report?"

He glanced down at the desk, lightly tapping the stack of papers of her analysis he'd printed out earlier.

"Your summary was more than sufficient for me to be confident in my earlier decision," he said as he took his forefinger and drew slow circles. Her eyes followed the movement and he bit back a smile, slowing the circles down to long strokes.

She licked her lips and shifted in her chair. Her blazer dipped open, and he could see the tight buds of her nipples pressing against her shirt.

Gorgeous.

He could see the slight patterning of lace beneath the fabric, and smiled knowing how the additional friction must feel against her flesh.

She cleared her throat, before speaking.

"Thank you," she said. "It took some extra digging, but all the evidence is there."

"Yes, I reviewed the report in depth earlier. But that's not what I wanted you here to discuss."

"It's not?"

"No. I hope you don't have any other plans this evening, because this may take a while."

"I-I have no other plans," she said.

"Good."

She clenched her hands in her lap and shifted again— uncrossing her legs before tilting them and crossing them again with the opposite leg.

He licked his lips at the thought of her naked and wet beneath her skirt. What would it take to have her admit that to him? His muscles tightened in anticipation as he looked up and smiled at her—he was about to find out.

***

Jessica counted to ten in her head, trying hard not to give into the urge to shift in her seat again.

Every move Lucas made seemed designed to arouse her further and it thrilled her as much as it scared her. Already her body strained towards release. When he'd asked if she could stay longer than usual, she almost wept aloud.

I can do this.

Breathing deeply she tried to focus on Lucas' words.

"It's no secret that I'm extremely satisfied with your work," he said.

A flush of pride spread through her.

"Thank you," she said.

She had confidence in her skills and knew that she was good at her job, but that didn't stop her from appreciating praise—especially from Lucas.

He tapped the file folder lying on his desk—his short, buffed nails sliding across the smooth linen paper. She pulled her gaze away from the hypnotic swirling of his fingers and shifted in her seat once more.

"According to my files, your contract with me is up for review and renewal."

She nodded, surprised she'd forgotten the day was approaching. In only a few days, she would have been working for him for a full year.

"You've been an incredible asset to the company and exceeded my original expectations," he said glancing up to hold her gaze. "That isn't a surprise to me. However, it does present me with an interesting dilemma. I was really hoping I could terminate your contract today."

She nodded before his words sank all the way in.

Wait a minute.

"Excuse me?"

He grinned at her.

"I was hoping to have an excuse not to renew your contract," he repeated.

"I don't understand."

He leaned forward and placed an elbow on the desk surface, cradling his chin in his palm as he assessed her.

"Let me be blunt—"

"When are you not?" she asked, interrupting him.

Tilting his head in agreement, he continued.

"I don't have personal relationships with my employees, but today I find myself in a difficult situation because I'd like to have a personal relationship with you."

Her jaw went slack as she processed his words.

"Personal relationship?" she whispered, her mind still not wanting to understand him.

"Very."

She remained silent for a moment—equal parts, amused, confused and irked. It was one thing to fantasize about having sex with him, even now, her entire body was on fire because of him, but his less than smooth delivery left her cold.

"Is this your way of asking me out?" she asked.

"In a way."

"Well in a *way*, how about you be a little clearer," she said, sitting back and folding her arms across her chest.

He smiled at the irate look she had no doubt was crossing her face.

"I'm attracted to you and would like to pursue a relationship…with you." He said.

"And what does that have to do with my contract?"

She firmed her lips at the implications of his statement. Perhaps she'd misunderstood him.

"I have a firm rule of not dating any of my employees."

"And you'd like to date me," she said, stating the words—not asking.

"Precisely."

Right. It really was as bad as she thought. Why didn't any of the books she read, mention just how sleazy a situation like this would be? What sounded sexy and dominant in a book proved to come across as strangely icky in real life. Did he really have so much arrogance that he thought, she'd just jump in his lap in gratitude?

"I know what you're thinking," he said, leaning back in his chair and resting his hands on the armrests.

She raised an eyebrow at him.

"I seriously, doubt that."

He raised a hand in the air and pointed his index finger up.

"One, you're thinking it's presumptuous of me to assume, that just because I want a relationship with you that it means you would want the same."

Raising another finger in the air, he continued.

"Two, you're thinking this is an odd and somewhat sleazy way for me to go about the situation."

She let him continue, curious as to how far he would go. Raising a third finger, he smiled, his gaze never leaving hers.

"And last, that if you weren't such a lady you would've kicked my ass by now."

"You forgot a few more things," she said as he dropped his hand back down to his side.

"What's that?"

She leaned forward and kept her gaze firmly trained on his.

"That you're not only presumptuous for assuming I feel the same way, but also an arrogant and misogynistic jerk if you think that even if I did choose to enter into a relationship with you, that that would give you the right to terminate my contract."

She stood and dropped her hands, palms flat, onto the desk and leaned forward.

"And furthermore, considering the undoubtedly large amount of psychology books you've devoured in your lifetime, I'd hoped that you'd find a classier way of propositioning a woman. And don't get it twisted…I can kick your ass and still be a lady."

He sat back staring at her with a goofy grin on his face.

"Noted," he said.

"That's all you have to say?" she asked, incredulous at his calm demeanor.

He shrugged his shoulders and continued to stare at her.

"There's not much else for me to say at the moment. Not until you address the big pink and white, polka-dotted elephant in the room," he said.

"And that would be?" she asked between clenched teeth.

"This whole conversation is somewhat moot, if you're not interested in me as well. You can either turn me and my delicate sensibilities down gently—"

She let out a loud snort at his description.

Delicate my ass.

"Or," he continued. "Admit to a mutual attraction and agree to go out with me. Or lastly, you can ignore it all… Kicking my ass is optional."

She stood staring at him dumbstruck. She didn't see any lie or joke in his eyes, only clear sincerity.

What the hell?

"Are you familiar with the term 'deconstructed orgasm'?" he asked.

"Excuse me?" she asked, her voice coming out in an embarrassing squeak.

Her mind whirled at the constant change of subjects.

"Deconstructed orgasm," he said again, his gaze boring into her.

She cleared her throat.

Where is he going with this?

Was this whole thing just another one of his strange tests? Some new psych-like way of discussing sexual harassment? She looked around the room, half expecting to see a telltale flash of a blinking hidden camera or a Human Resources representative standing in the corner.

As many times as she'd fantasized about Lucas, not one fantasy involved him firing her and talking about orgasms.

Okay maybe the orgasms part—yes. But not the firing part.

Turning back to look at him, she was caught again in his golden gaze. Although his lips were curled up in good

34

humor, his eyes held a serious glint of sincerity that gave her pause. Clearing her throat, she attempted to appear unfazed.

"Maybe," she said, not wanting to admit she knew the term.

He titled his head in a mocking angle, but she didn't elaborate. She didn't know where this conversation was heading, but she sure as hell didn't plan to reveal any of her secrets during the course of it.

"A deconstructed orgasm is usually part of BDSM play—a type of play I like to engage in with my lovers," he said.

He paused for a moment and she stared blankly at him.

This is not happening.

She did *not* just hear Lucas say he liked BDSM. Shaking her head, she closed her eyes convinced she'd fallen into some strange dream.

"I'm a sadist Jessica," he said.

That statement snapped her out of her fog.

Not happening.

"I don't—"

He held up a hand interrupting her.

"I'm not a whips and chains kind of man," he said. "The type of play I like to indulge in involves denial."

She froze.

"Denial?" she asked, whispering out the all too familiar word.

He nodded.

"I prefer what some people call orgasm denial. I enjoy performing extended acts of foreplay—of having a woman give me the pleasure of denying her of her own," he said.

"Why are you telling me this?"

"Because I believe in being honest and letting any potential partners know what I like…And because I believe you might crave exactly what I have to offer."

She shook her head in denial.

"I'd believe you more if you hadn't walked in here looking like you weren't desperate to come," he whispered. "If I didn't see the same desire and curiosity I have for you reflected in your eyes each time I see you."

She stumbled back at his worlds, unable to voice a denial or affirmation.

"I'm not saying any of this to be cruel," he continued.

"Then why are you?" she asked, her shoulders stiff.

With a few short words, he'd exposed a secret craving—one she was still struggling to come to grips with herself. However, even as she stood there, her private thoughts exposed, she couldn't keep from wanting to know more.

"What exactly are you asking for?" she asked.

"I'm asking for one night. One night to indulge in the fantasies we both have…in the flesh."

His shadowed gaze filled with heat as he visually traced the shape of her mouth causing a slow burn to rekindle in her body. He touched the folder on the desk and slid it towards her.

"For you," he said.

She eyed the document, unsure of what it might contain.

"I swear to God, if this is some kind of weird sex contract I'll hurt you,"

He threw back his head and laughed.

"Who the hell types up a sex contract?" he asked when his mirth finally subsided.

"You'd be surprised," she said, still not picking up the papers.

"Well rest assured that document contains nothing about sex. But if you'd like I can always have it amended."

He waggled his eyebrows at her.

Frowning, she refused to feel embarrassed. He was the one who had brought sex and BDSM into their conversation in the first place.

Giving into curiosity, she reached for the folder and flipped it open. Nestled in its center was her renewal contract. Surprise stiffened her shoulders and she glanced up at him in question.

He greeted her look with silence and one arrogantly raised eyebrow.

Looking back down she flipped through the document, stopping to read key paragraphs. The document not only offered a renewal of her contract for an additional five years, but also gave her a hefty salary increase and a bonus for every year she chose to remain with the company. What astounded her even more was the small elegant scrawl at the bottom of each page and the bold signature on the final page.

"You were right. I would never expect you to give up your position because I'm attracted to you," he said when she raised her startled gaze to his.

"That contract is iron clad," he continued. "Regardless of what your decision is today, your job is secure. The only question now is whether you choose to sign it and stay here with me tonight, or sign it and pretend this conversation never happened. And before you question the salary or the bonuses—they have nothing to do with my proposition. You're an asset to this company. I'm only paying you what you deserve."

Unable to focus on the full implication of his statement, she narrowed her eyes at him and responded to the only thing she knew with certainty.

"Of course I'm worth it. You'd be an idiot not offer me competitive compensation. You're just lucky your benefits plan is so great or I would insist on more."

"I stand corrected."

She frowned at him—upset that he'd thrown her for a loop yet again. It had been so much easier to be upset when he behaved like a sleaze, yet now he had her seriously considering his offer.

In a way, it would kill two birds with one stone. Not only would she get to test out her fantasies of Lucas in real life, but she'd also get to have a true D/s experience that catered to her need for denial.

"The choice still remains up to you," he said. "There are two bedrooms in this suite. All I'm asking for is one night to get to know you better and if at the end of the night you choose not to sleep with me, you go to your room and I'll go to mine. I won't pursue you further. In the morning Eli will take you back to your hotel and the next time we meet we can pretend it never happened."

His words shivered through her. Did she dare?

He'd offered her everything she wanted on a platter—the chance to play, to see if her feelings for him were real, but did she really want to know?

Closing her eyes briefly, she made her decision.

She opened her eyes and found Lucas staring at her intently. Her body trembled at the heated promise of his gaze.

Bending slightly she picked up her purse and tucked the contract in the front compartment.

"Which room is mine?" she asked.

A broad smile stretched his lips at her question.

"The left," he said, pointing to the solitary door on the opposite side of the room.

"I have early dinner reservations scheduled for six and tickets to a show a little later. The closet is also stocked with anything you might need," he said as she retreated.

She paused and turned her head, looking at him over her shoulder.

"You were that sure of yourself?"

"Not sure—hopeful," he replied.

So am I.

She pulled open the bedroom door and hesitated before stepping over the threshold.

So am I.

Stepping into the room, she closed the door firmly behind her.

Four

LUCAS COULDN'T KEEP his eyes off Jessica.

Her silky skin glowed under the soft lighting in the candlelit restaurant. The loose bun she'd styled at her nape accentuated the elegant line of her neck. It was different from her usual tight buns or ponytails. He wondered what her hair would look like free and flowing. Would it graze along her delicate collarbone or curl along her chest?

He slid his gaze over her bare shoulders, pausing a moment to rest on the lush cleavage displayed by the light-purple, corseted top of her dress. Every time she took a breath he held in his own in stark appreciation of the gorgeous curves on display.

"You're staring," she said.

He brought his gaze up to her face.

"You look beautiful," he said. "I was just appreciating the view."

"You were *appreciating* my boobs," she said, reaching out to take a sip of water.

"That's what I said." He grinned at her, hoping to ease some of the tension holding her body stiff.

She fidgeted across from him, her nervousness written clear across her face. Her discomfort, made him glad he'd chosen to dine at the hotel restaurant instead of having dinner sent to the suite.

"It's rude," she murmured.

He snorted at her response.

"Like how you checked out my ass before I sat down?"

Her eyes widened.

"How did you—"

She snapped her lips shut when he began to chuckle.

"I didn't, but I do now."

She picked up her napkin and tossed it at him, a small smile twitching across her lips. He caught it in mid-air, happy to see her begin to relax.

After a few more minutes, he was able to coax her into an easy conversation. By the time their dinner arrived, she seemed more at ease.

"Tell me about your family," he said.

She shrugged her shoulders, picked up her fork and idly began moving food around on her plate.

"There's not much to tell. I'm an only child. I grew up in New York, went to college, and became an actuary. Pretty boring stuff," she said before spearing a carrot and bringing it to her mouth.

He watched her closely, noting the stiff set of her shoulders. She chewed her food slowly, her features blank.

"What about your parents?"

She froze before, swallowing her food and reaching for her glass of wine.

"They're no longer in the picture," she said after taking a sip.

"I'm sorry, my condolences," he murmured.

He and his parents were extremely close and he couldn't imagine what it would be like to lose both of them.

She set her glass down and let out a snort.

"They're not dead—they're in Morocco," she said, her lips twisted in a sardonic smile.

"Somehow I get the feeling they're not there on vacation," he said.

"Bingo."

"My extreme powers of insight are also telling me that you don't want to talk about it."

She leaned back in her chair and stared at him for a moment.

"There really isn't that much to tell. Both of my parents grew up around a lot of money, but they never learned how to come by it honestly themselves. When I was thirteen they fled the country after my father got caught embezzling from his investment firm."

"And they didn't take you with them?"

She shrugged her shoulders again.

"I chose to stay behind. I knew my parents well enough by then to see the writing on the wall. I may have had dreams of traveling, but none of them involved running from the law."

"That's a young age to be on your own," he said frowning.

What type of parents would just abandon their child like that?

Bastards.

"Relax Dr. Phil. I went to live with my grandparents. My father's parents died before I was born, but my grandparents on my mother's side are still alive and well. I stayed with them until I left for college."

He did relax at the fond expression softening her face. However she felt about her parents, it was obvious that she held affection for her grandparents.

"You're close," he said, smiling at her.

"Yes," she replied, her smile stretching wider. "They're a little eccentric, but were great parents to me."

"How eccentric?"

Her eyes twinkled back at him.

"My grand dad is an inventor. He made his fortune by patenting some computer chip design. He's tried to explain it to me a million times, but it still all sounds like gibberish. Anyway, he has a lab set up in the basement and he likes to tinker as he puts it. I can't tell you how many times he convinced our cook to try some new gadget, or how many times my car wouldn't start because he had to *borrow* a part for whatever project he was working on at the time."

He chuckled at her description.

"What about your grandmother?"

"Ah. Gran is just as much of a free spirit. She's an artist. I don't think there's ever been a time when she hasn't had paint under nails or smeared on her clothes. She's very good though."

"Would I be familiar with any of her work?"

"Maybe," she said, reaching for her glass again.

He narrowed his eyes at the grin she tried to hide behind her drink.

"What's your grandmother's name?" he asked.

She cleared her throat before speaking.

"Elizabeth Francis."

His jaw dropped open at the name. Not only was he familiar with the famous artist's work he owned several of her paintings. One of them in particular hung over the mantle in his bedroom back home in Chicago.

His gaze dropped to take in the curve of Jessica's neck and lush flare of her breasts and a puzzle piece clicked into place.

"You're Calypso," he whispered, still stunned at his revelation.

Her smile dimmed at his words.

"You've seen that painting?"

"I *own* that painting," he said.

It was her turn to look taken aback. Her eyes widened in a startled gaze, before closing her eyes and shaking her head.

"Oh my God," she muttered.

He threw back his head and laughed. He couldn't help it.

"Look at it this way," he said "Now that I've seen you naked the ice is officially broken."

She picked up her napkin and tossed it at him again, her expression still embarrassed.

"It's not funny."

"Oh come on. You have to admit that it's at least a little bit funny."

"Not in this life time."

"Will it help if we change the subject?" he asked still grinning.

"Infinitely."

He spread his hands wide.

"I'm an open book. Ask me anything."

She eyed him for a moment before nodding. They talked about his family and his own childhood growing up with two academically minded parents.

The conversation eventually shifted to other topics. From books to music, he was surprised to learn just how much they had in common, but where they disagreed, she had no qualms in sharing and defending her opinion. It only confirmed for him how well suited they were for each other. As the meal progressed, he couldn't help but fall a little harder for her.

The more he learned about her, the more he realized his gut had been right along. Jessica Sinclair was his perfect match.

They were enjoying dessert when he saw the small shift in her demeanor.

"What is it?" he asked.

He could see the wheels of indecision in her eyes, before she firmed her lips and responded.

"This," she said, waving her fork in the air and gesturing at the table and the restaurant.

"What do you really want from me?" she asked.

He'd known she would ask eventually. Lucky for him he already had an answer.

"Everything."

She licked her lips at his answer.

"That's a pretty broad answer."

"Maybe, but it's true."

He reached across the table and placed his hand over hers, stroking the smooth softness of her skin with his thumb.

"I don't do casual relationships—not anymore. I wouldn't have offered this proposal to you if all I wanted were to fuck you. Which I really want to do by the way. In every sweaty way imaginable."

Her eyes dilated at his words, the warm brown darkening to black.

"I'm honest enough with myself to let you know that I've developed feelings for you. I wouldn't have suggested this night if I didn't, but I also want to help you explore sexual denial. To help you determine if it's something you really want."

He knew her next question before she asked.

"What do I have to do?" she asked finally.

"Gift me absolute control of your pleasure tonight. Let me show you how good the game can be when you submit."

His cocked stirred at the anticipation and desire stamped across her features. The emotion burned bright in her eyes as she stared back at him. He remained silent, allowing her time to make a decision. After a few moments, she turned her palm up into his and twined her fingers with his.

"Okay," she said softly.

Five

JESSICA'S PULSE RACED as she stepped into the limo, slid along the smooth leather seats and waited for Lucas to join her. Dinner had proved to be enlightening. On one level, she felt more comfortable with Lucas than ever before, but also more confused. He'd said that he had feelings for her and she puzzled over that.

Did that mean they shared the same dilemma? Did he worry that his feelings would wane compared to the reality of her as well?

She had hoped this night would give her some clarity, but instead of finding distance between him and her fantasy man, she kept on finding too many similarities. Even worse was that the reality was proving to be much better.

She frowned a bit at the thought. Perhaps that wasn't entirely true. Lucas had shown that on a personal level, he could compete, but so far, they hadn't even kissed. For all she knew, his talk was just that.

Licking her lips, she recalled what he said at dinner and stared at the bench of seating opposite her. Was she willing to take their games further?

She could hear him just outside the door speaking to Eli. With her heart pounding a loud tattoo in her ears, she shifted to the opposite bench. She'd just crossed her legs and settled back in the seat when the door opened and Lucas climbed into the car—his long tuxedo clad limbs folding and uncoiling in fluid movements as he settled onto his seat.

No surprise registered on his face as he looked at her. Instead, a small smile worked his lips as his gaze wandered up her body starting from the tips of her silver shoes. She felt it like a caress on her skin moving up inch by inch. By the time his eyes met hers she couldn't contain the shiver that slithered down her spine.

"I see you're ready to play," he said.

She clenched fists at her side and nodded.

"You did say twenty-four hours," she said.

His only reply was a wicked grin. She heard Eli climb into the car and slam the door shut. The soft purr of the engine vibrated in the air. Holding her breath, she waited for Lucas' next move.

He didn't disappoint. She had no doubt that he knew that the anticipation drove her crazy. She locked her muscles against the need to squirm in her seat, but the longer he stared at her, the more her skin tingled sending prickles of heat to skitter down her body and pool at her center.

She muffled a soft sigh as he reached forward and pressed a small button on the center console. A compartment slid open. Inside was an ice bucket with champagne and two champagne flutes.

"I think this is cause for celebration," he said as he pulled the bottle free.

He peeled the gold foil back from the top of the bottle.

"What are we celebrating?" She asked.

"Pleasure," he said.

The loud popping of the cork filled the air. Her gaze followed the trail of fizzy bubbles flow from its top. The liquid foam trickled onto his hands as he poured the bubbly wine into each flute. She swallowed hard against the need to follow the effervescent trail with her tongue.

He placed the bottle back on the ice before pulling the two flutes free. His gaze kept her captive as he offered the glass to her.

It was as if he was issuing another challenge. She reached forward and took the drink from his hand, her fingertips brushing against his. Pulling in a deep breath, she steadied her trembling hand before leaning back into her seat.

Even now, without saying more than a few words to her she was on edge. As if knowing exactly what she was thinking he raised his glass in the air in a toast.

"Cheers," he said.

Her stomach clenched in excitement. Despite his nonchalance, she could tell that he was just as on edge as she was.

"Cheers."

She tilted her head back and took a deep swig of the fizzy liquid. The cool bubbles tripped down her throat and tickled her nose. She welcomed the slight distraction. On some level, she loved how quickly her body responded to him, but tonight was different. Tonight the internal games she played with herself were real.

His gaze slid down her body again in one long lazy stroke before looking back up into her eyes.

"I hope you like the opera," he said.

"Is that where we're going tonight?"

"Yes. I thought you'd enjoy an opera playing at the Adrienne Arscht."

She nodded and took another sip of her champagne, recognizing the name of the sleek opera house in Miami.

"I haven't been to too many operas. The language barrier has always been an issue."

"I think you'll find this one interesting."

"Really?"

"Yes. It's one of the few operas originally written to be performed in English."

She raised a brow at the glint of amusement in his eyes.

"Something tells me there's more to it than that," she said.

He threw his head back and laughed.

"And you'd be right," he said, "It's a British piece and relatively new as operas go, but it's been surrounded by its fair share of controversy."

"Why?" She asked.

His cheeks dimpled again in a wicked smile.

"I think I'll leave that part a surprise."

He changed the subject, alternating between serious issues to more mundane topics at will—each switch in conversation a direct contrast to the anticipation building in her body. Trying to distract herself and slow her mounting excitement, she glanced out of the window and watched the city landscape pass by. It had been almost five years since she'd last visited South Florida, but she still recalled the layout well. It would be at least another half hour before they reached the opera house in the outskirts of Downtown Miami. Her stomach clenched at the amount of time stretching before her.

Does he know? He must.

With each shift in conversation, she became flushed with a combination of anticipation and disappointment. The two warring emotions swirled in her, making it difficult for her to concentrate. She was too eager to see what game Lucas would initiate.

She gripped the glass in her hand, raised it to her lips for another sip, and was surprised to realize the flute was already empty.

"Another?"

She hesitated for a moment before nodding and stretching her arm out for more. She didn't want to overindulge but felt a little extra liquid courage might help calm her nerves. Lucas picked up the champagne bottle and refilled her glass.

Murmuring her thanks, she took a slow sip, focusing on relaxing her muscles and slowing her racing pulse.

Lucas continued speaking. She didn't bother trying to follow along any longer. She had long since lost track of the conversation. Shifting slightly in her seat, she noticed his gaze flicker down to her chest. She glanced down at her dress and realized the movement had caused the corset portion of her gown to push her cleavage up even more.

Bingo.

She wasn't the only one enjoying and suffering in the car. Lucas was just as aware of the tension as she was, but he seemed content on letting it simmer.

She didn't want simmering, she wanted a blazing fire and he'd said he wanted her to give him control. Maybe it was time for her to show him she was ready.

She placed the champagne flute down on the console before crossing her arms under her breasts, she smiled as his eyes took on a dark hooded quality. She shifted again and slowly uncrossed her legs, keeping them close together before tilting them to the side and crossing them again in the opposite direction.

His speech slowly trailed off to a stop. She couldn't resist the urge to smile in triumph, but her victory was short-lived.

He raised his smoldering gaze to hers and she could see the decision in his eyes. Whatever button she had just pressed, ignited the starting flare.

Let the games begin.

This is what she wanted.

When he leaned back in the soft leather, she felt a tinge of disappointment. For the first time since she'd met him, she'd let impatience rule her actions. She loved anticipation but now wondered whether winning would be as satisfying.

"Don't worry. We have plenty of time," he said.

She furrowed her brow at this statement.

What does that mean?

"The key strategy in winning any game is knowing your opponent," he said.

"So you admit this is a game?" She asked.

"Of course, one that we've both been playing since the day we met. The only difference is that now we both know what the prize is."

"And that would be…"

She knew the answer. They both did, but she wanted to hear him say it.

"I get to win and you get to lose."

She sucked in a breath at that.

"That doesn't sound like much of a prize."

He kept his gaze firmly trained on her; his intense stare holding her captive.

"It's the reward we both want."

"How do you figure that?" she asked.

He took another sip of champagne before answering.

"The Redford case."

His three simple words landed between them like a gauntlet. Her already sensitized skin tingled with new awareness.

He knew. She could see it in his eyes.

Several months ago she'd investigated a firm in San Francisco—Redford Mechanics. The case had gone relatively smooth but she knew that wasn't what Lucas was referring to.

He'd been out of the country when she finished the case and it was several weeks before she was able to meet him in person. It was the first time since she began working for him that she hadn't been able to see him immediately after closing up a file. That hadn't stopped her from playing out her fantasies, from touching and teasing herself every night until she saw him again. It was the longest bout of denial she'd ever experienced. By the time she'd finally been able to schedule an appointment with him the anticipation had built up inside her to a point of almost madness.

Before leaving for his office, she'd reached under her skirt and slipped off her panties, shuffling them in her desk drawer before making her way down the long hallway to his large office.

By the time she sat across from him at his desk, her thighs were wet with her own arousal. She'd sat in that meeting listening to his husky voice, each melodic timber bringing her closer and closer to the brink. When the meeting was over and he escorted her to the door, she was trembling. His shoulder grazed across her chest as he leaned forward to open the door. She'd gasped aloud and stumbled back, her already hardened nipples stiffening further to an almost painful degree. He'd murmured a quick question asking if she was okay. Even now she couldn't recall what she said, only that her response must of satisfied his curiosity because he stepped away enough for her to leave.

That was the only time he ever broke her restraint.

She'd barely made it back to her office in time before she slammed the door shut, lifted her skirt and slid her fingers into the hot, wet folds of her pussy. Leaning against the door, she bit her bottom lip to muffle the sound of her moans as she circled her clit once, twice. She exploded and clenched her thighs tight around her hand before she even completed the third stroke.

"You remember," he said now with a smile.

"What exactly am I supposed to be remembering?" she asked.

"That I'm an incredibly observant man," he said.

She remained silent.

"Nothing to say?" he asked.

Licking her lips, she shook her head.

"Excellent."

He leaned forward in his seat, resting his elbows on his knees, the hand holding his drink dangling down his leg.

"Show me," he said.

His husky demand rocked her. Did she dare?

"We can always not play," he said at her hesitation.

No!

Her heart lurched at that possibility. As much as their new game challenged her, she didn't want it to end. Instead, she licked her lips and held his gaze. It wasn't difficult. When he was near she remained caught in a strange web of want and greedy expectation controlled only by him.

She unfolded her arms and placed her hands at her sides, curling her fingers tight into her palms. The small bite of her nails digging into her skin helped ground her. Slowly, she uncrossed her legs and pressed her knees tightly together.

His gaze didn't flicker downward to look, the golden flecks in his eyes seemed to glow and held her transfixed.

"Show me," he said again.

Taking a deep, shaky breath, she unfurled her fingers and clenched the smooth satin of her skirt before pulling it up her thighs, inch by inch before settling the bunched material at her hips.

"More."

At his husky demand, she spread her legs open, exposing her secret to him, feeling the cool caress of air drift over her naked sex. His gaze didn't waver—it didn't dip down to see what she offered to him.

"Perfect. Now isn't that better?"

She nodded at a loss for words. She did feel better. Something about exposing herself to him—of them both being fully aware of her eagerness to please, ratcheted up her need to another notch.

"Good," he said. "I remember that day so clearly. It was the first time I've ever seen you so distracted. Your eyes were glassy and bright. But you know what tipped me off to your naughty little secret?" he asked.

She licked her lips unsure of how to answer.

"You kept squirming in your chair crossing and uncrossing your legs and every now and then you would let out a sexy sigh. That's when I knew and I wanted to see how long you could last like that. What it would take to break you? That was the day I realized we'd both been playing the same game all along."

He took another sip of his drink, a small smile playing across his lips.

"I'd wondered about it for a while which is why extended my business trip. I wanted to see if our meetings where as stimulating to you as they were to me."

She clenched her hands tighter, her breath coming out in deep pants. She wanted him to look at her, to slide his hot gaze down to her center and see how wet and ready she was for him. He didn't. Lucas continued to speak as if she wasn't open and bared to him.

"Another test?" she asked, her voice sounding wispy and thin to her ears.

He nodded.

"In a way. That's when I realized that you and I could be great together. I loved watching you squirm, loved knowing that you sat there with your wet, creaming pussy, and that it was all for me. But most of all I enjoyed denying you that release, of knowing the pain of denial was bringing us both so much pleasure."

She couldn't refute the truth in his words, even now as he spoke to her, ignoring her splayed legs, he kept her on edge.

"I've always known that I'm a bit of a sadist," he said. "But I've never been into physical pain. I've never wanted to whip a woman or spank her until she begged—although I can see the merits in that. My weakness has always been in denial, in a woman giving me ultimate control of her body and arousal, allowing me to determine when and where she gets to come."

"That day in my office I realized you wanted the same things. You were bringing yourself to the edge of orgasm all because we were both denying you pleasure. If I'm a bit of a sadist Jessica, you are most definitely a masochist."

"Then what does that make us?" she asked.

A dimple flashed on his cheek as he smirked at her.

"A perfect match," he said.

Her breath hitched as his eyes finally broke contact with hers. His gaze slipped with deliberate slowness down her body. She knew where it rested at each moment—a languid caress at her breasts, a lingering stroke at her navel. When it finally dipped down between her legs, she closed her eyes on a groan.

Her stomach clenched and her core creamed as his gaze lingered there.

Yes.

With just one look, her clit throbbed and her pussy clenched, eager for release. But it wasn't enough. Opening her eyes she watched him stare down at her open cunt— wanting to know his next move. Breathing in heavy gasps, she felt the moment he looked away, felt the delicious slide of his gaze work its way back up her body. When he looked into her eyes again, her heart stuttered to a stop for a split moment before galloping fast in earnest again. His golden eyes were like twin flames staring back at her, mirroring the intense need burning through her.

"Beautiful," he murmured.

She wanted to close her eyes again at his husky praise, but his every movement kept her enthralled.

"Would you like me to touch you there?"

Yes.

She nodded, but just as quickly shook her head. She wanted him to do both. She wanted him to deny her and give her pleasure all at once. The warring emotions held her still and only seemed to make her want him more.

"I won't do anything until you ask me first."

Her hands crushed the material of her skirt. Her entire body throbbed, shaking with arousal and indecision.

"Maybe I should tell you what I want to do while you make up your mind," he said.

She groaned as he placed his flute down, and dropped to his knees on the floor of the limo.

In long, lithe movements, he crawled to her, his expression full of wicked intent. Even when his head was level with her core, he didn't move his eyes away from hers.

Whimpering she shook harder and spread her thighs wider, wanting his scalding gaze back on her pulsing sex.

"I want to dip my tongue in that dripping pussy of yours and drown in all that sweetness," he said before rising to his knees and placing his hands on her thighs.

Her skin sizzled where he touched her, as if he was branding her with his dirty words.

"I want to eat you for hours and see how many times I can make you burst and come all over me," he said, moving his thumbs in slow circles on her inner thighs as he tilted his head down and touched his mouth to hers.

"I want to hold you wide open and see how long and hard I can fuck you until you scream my name," he whispered against her lips.

He nibbled his way down her jaw and nuzzled her neck, his tongue licking hot flames across her skin.

"Now…do you have an answer to my question, Jessica? Do you want me to touch your pretty pussy?"

Letting out a loud groan, she shrieked her answer.

"Yes!"

His hot tongue licked the shell of her ear, before his husky voice whispered to her.

"No."

Six

THEIR TREK THROUGH the crowded opera house was a blur. Jessica used the time to collect her senses, not bothering to note the names on the marquee or playbills littered throughout the hall. She couldn't even recall how she made it into the theater. Only Lucas' hot words played through her mind.

I want to hold you wide open and see how long and hard I can fuck you until you scream my name.

Every word he'd spoken pushed her to a different level of desire she'd never felt before.

His sexy words had set her ablaze but none of them ignited her like his last.

No.

Such a simple word, but spoken in his deep voice, knowing that she was only a single stroke away from coming was the most delicious thing she'd ever heard. Even now, her pussy throbbed at the knowledge that his fingers had been so close to sliding in between her wet folds, but not close enough. It was official.

I'm in lust with a sadist.

She shivered. Prickling goose bumps rushed across her skin, flushing her with heat and confusion all at once. As it stood, it took all of her effort to walk a straight line. If it weren't for Lucas' hand at her back guiding her through the crowd and up the curving flight of stairs to the private boxes, she would've melted into a puddle on the floor. However, each step brought back a small measure of sanity and control. By the time they entered the private opera box the hot blaze Lucas had ignited in her body down in the limo had cooled to a low simmer.

Helping her into her seat, his hands lingered on her bare shoulders for a short moment before he slid into the chair next to hers.

They remained silent. She knew it was only a slight reprieve but welcomed it nonetheless. As much as he gave her choices, it had become obvious that Lucas planned to push her to her limits.

Reaching up a shaky hand, she smoothed her fingers over her hair making sure to tuck in any loose strands. The small ritual helped sooth her further.

Glancing around, she began to register the excellent view their seats provided. The theater was shaped in a narrow "U" formation with the stage centered at its opening. Their seats were just left of the base of the shape, giving them a clear bird's eye view of the stage as well as the audience watching. The soft sounds of instruments tuning filled the air just under the din of voices from the mingling crowd.

She'd always loved to people watch and she'd forgotten just how entertaining a Miami crowd could be. People from all walks of life, and in various forms of dress milled around searching for their seats. Some were in simple jeans and t-shirts—the obvious college crowd. Others wore the typical business suits and harried looks of people arriving straight from work. While others were like her, dressed formally in evening dress.

She scanned the crowd of the poshly dressed, knowing that in Miami there'd be more than one celebrity out for an evening of enjoyment. She located a few politicians and several actors before her gaze settled on the box directly opposite hers in the theater.

A woman stood at the entrance of the box, stunning in a full-length nude colored gown, embroidered with crystal sequins. Her long blonde hair fell over one shoulder, the golden locks curling at her breast and tipped in bright pink. Jessica recognized the woman immediately as a famous pop singer known for being equal parts demure and risqué. The woman stepped inside the box, and flanking her sides were two handsome, tall men.

"Is that?"

"Are you referring to the woman or the men?" Lucas asked, following the direction of her gaze.

"The woman. Is that who I think she is?"

"The singer? Yes," he said. "I should have known they wouldn't be able to resist this show."

"You know them?"

"I know the two men. They're Italian businessmen—best friends in fact. I've run into them a time or two."

"What did you mean they wouldn't be able to resist the show?"

"Alfonse and Nico can never resist showing off a new pet," he said. "You'll figure it out soon enough."

Jessica stared across the audience at the beautiful trio. The men were both very handsome, their dark looks flanking the curvaceous blonde like sexy bookends. Her pale looks and nude colored gown contrasted nicely with their deep olive skin tone and dark suits.

They settled onto their seats, the woman sitting between them. The man to the right, draped an arm over the singer's shoulder and caressed the skin exposed by the thin straps of her dress. The woman smiled and turned her head to give the man a lingering kiss. Jessica watched as they kissed, the man's hand sliding down the singer's shoulder-dragging the strap of her gown down with it. The dress dipped down and one pink-tipped breast popped free.

Jessica gasped at the sight, amazed at the open display of lust and sexuality. Her surprise turned to outright astonishment when a dark hand reached up and began to fondle the woman's breast. The hand didn't belong to the man kissing her, but to the other man sitting at the singer's left. He cupped the firm globe in his hand smoothing his thumb back and forth across the rosy nub.

"Are they…"

"Yes,"

She glanced around the audience, curious to see if anyone one else witnessed the provocative display of flesh and sensuality. How could no one else be staring?

"The seats in the private boxes are slightly recessed and angled. The only people who can see in this light are those performing on the stage and us," Lucas said as if reading her mind.

The lights in the theater began to dim and the trio in the opposite box slowly faded from view—their sexual play marked by faint wisps of shadow. Leaning forward, her eyes strained against the darkness wanting to see more.

"The show is about to begin," Lucas said, a tinge of amusement marking his voice.

"I thought I was already watching one," she whispered back to him.

He chuckled softly.

"Don't worry, this one won't disappoint."

The orchestra started playing—a jazzy tune resembling a big band ensemble filled the air. The stage lit and a spotlight shone on a woman sitting at a small vanity mirror in the center of the stage. An actress dressed as a maid sat nearby on a bed, staring at the other woman.

Even with Lucas' previous warning, Jessica was pleasantly surprised when the woman began to sing in clear English.

"What's the name of this opera again?" she whispered.

"Powder Her Face."

As the show progressed, Jessica realized exactly why Lucas thought the opera would appeal to her. The main character, the Duchess of Argyll was scandalous in her sexual adventures and exploits. Moreover, not to be left out, the supporting cast participated in a few scandalous scenes of their own.

By the time the curtain dropped for intermission, Jessica was thoroughly engaged in the plot and its characters.

When the lights dimmed up, she turned to Lucas with a wide smile.

"I take it you're enjoying yourself?" he asked returning her smile with a grin of his own.

"Yes," she said. "I never knew opera could be so raunchy."

He let out a husky laugh.

"Wait until you see the second act, there's rumor of a pretty graphic fellatio scene."

"*No!*"

She stared at him wide eyed for a moment before bursting into laughter.

"I think you've just converted me to high theater," she said in between snickers.

A small knock sounded at the door behind them before a waiter stepped into the box offering drinks. Forgoing another glass of champagne, they both chose water. When the door shut behind the retreating server, she settled back into her seat and took a long sip of the crisp water.

Glancing back to the stage she wondered how much longer before the show resumed.

"Too bad this isn't like the old drive in movies," she said. "You know—how they would play little cartoons during intermission."

"If you're looking for entertainment you only have to look in the box in front of us. Your little singer seems to be enjoying her visit to the opera...a lot."

Jessica's head whipped around at his statement. During the course of the show, she'd completely forgotten about the sexy ménage.

Her gaze landed on the other box and widened.

Good Lord.

The singer still sat in her chair facing forward, but this time Jessica saw only one man in the box. He stood behind the woman's chair, his lips nibbling her throat and both of his hands kneading her exposed breasts.

Suddenly a third hand slid up the woman's torso and Jessica knew without a doubt where the second man had disappeared to.

Jessica's breath caught in her throat at the carnal sight.

"I wonder what he's doing down there?"

She jumped at the Lucas' voice. His chest grazed her shoulder as he leaned over and whispered into her ear.

"Maybe he heard about act two and the spirit moved him."

"Oh God."

"I'm pretty sure that's exactly what she'd saying right now," he said. "Look at her chest heaving up and down, the way she's moving her head from left to right."

Lucas, rested a hand on her thigh, and with that small gesture, she recalled their encounter in the limo and her body flared back into overdrive.

"I can't say that I blame him," Lucas continued.

"I know what it's like to be starved for a taste of something. To want to hold a bowl of cream to my mouth and lick it clean."

Jessica shuddered out a breath at his heated words.

"You're really good at this you know?"

She felt his lips spread in a smile at her nape.

"No—just damn determined to savor my dessert."

The lights in the hall began to dim again, and Lucas leaned back into his seat, but kept his hand splayed across her upper right thigh.

Several long minutes passed before Jessica got her breathing under control and she turned her attention back to the stage.

This is going to be a long night.

Seven

JESSICA TREMBLED AS she slid onto the back seat of the limo. She'd remained on edge throughout the rest of the second act. Lucas had been right about it— the second act was just as salacious as the first, and knowing that even more carnal acts were occurring in the shadowed box just across the way, kept her in a constant state of arousal.

By the time the final curtain fell, she thought she'd reached a maximum until Lucas leaned over and whispered in her ear.

"When we get to the car I want you to pull up your skirt and spread those gorgeous legs for me."

The wicked request had her shaking. She'd wanted nothing more than to stay where she sat and pull her skirt up right then and there. Before she could voice her opinion on the matter, Lucas helped her from her seat and led her from the theater.

Now all she could think of was his mouth sliding against her moist flesh. Breathing heavily she stared at him as he slid into the seat next to her.

The moment the limo door shut, she yanked up her skirt and spread her legs wide.

"Please," she whispered, not caring how desperate she looked or sounded.

Lucas smiled and let out a grunt of approval, but he didn't obey her frenzied demand. Instead, he dropped to the floor and knelt between her knees.

He cupped the cheeks of her face and tilted her head up to meet his smoldering gaze.

"I'm in charge remember? I determine when and how we play," he said.

She almost sobbed at his reminder.

"Yes," she whispered, giving him the control he demanded.

A wicked glint lit his eyes and he responded.

"Good."

Releasing her face, he slid his palms down her shoulders and caressed her arms for a moment before sliding his hands onto her torso.

She whimpered when he tugged the bodice of her dress down, exposing her breasts to the cool air.

"I like it when you whimper," he said, his fingers lightly stroking the flesh just above her areola.

"It makes me wonder what other sounds you'll make when I take you."

His hands slid down again, each one cupping a breast and squeezing, before stroking a thumb just below her aching nipple.

She squirmed in his arms unable to hold back another whimper. She desperately wanted him to ease the need building inside her, but she craved the tortuously slow burn he stoked with his teasing caresses.

"You're not playing fair," she said.

He chuckled—the sound vibrating across her skin.

"We never talked about fair," he said.

Her shriek of frustration quickly turned to a low moan as he released her breasts and captured her nipples in a tight pinch between his fingers.

"I like that sound too," he said.

He dropped his hands to her thighs, leaned down and swirled his hot tongue around one throbbing peak.

At her responding groan, he opened his mouth wide, sucking the engorged bud hard. She raised her hands to his head holding him tight to her chest.

She undulated beneath him, wanting to pull him closer—wanting to wrap her legs around him and roughly rub against his cock, but his fingers tightened on her thighs keeping her firmly in place, reminding her that everything would be at his leisure.

His mouth left her breast after one long lingering lick. He smoothed his hands under her thighs, yanked her to the edge of the seat and settled down onto the backs of his feet, staring hotly at her center.

She spread her legs wider, eager to feel whatever torture he planned next.

He licked his lips before reaching out with one finger and sliding it down her center.

They both groaned aloud at the slippery contact. She canted her hips upward wanting more.

"So perfect," he whispered.

His finger circled her clit before sliding down her slit and dipping inside just a fraction.

"I can't wait to take you here," he said. "To feel you stretched tight all around me."

Flicking his gaze back up to hers, he smiled.

"Do you want that?" he asked.

She nodded frantically, unable to speak.

"Good, but for now I'll have to satisfy myself with a little taste."

He slipped his finger from her core and dragged it back up through her folds, before bringing it up to his lips. He sucked the finger into his mouth, licking it clean of her juices. The act held her in agonizing attention.

She wanted his mouth on her, wanted him to lick her pussy with the same eagerness he gave to his finger. With one final lick, he dropped his hand and rose to stand on his knees again.

She moaned in protest, thinking it was the end of their game, but he reached for her instead, wrapping his arms around her and pulling her tight.

The move brought her pussy flush against his thick cock. Even through his layers of clothing, she could feel its heat.

"Stay still," he warned as if knowing exactly what she was thinking.

He buried a hand at the nape of her neck and began to tug at the pins that held her hair in place. After a few moments, her hair tumbled free—thick and curling around her shoulders.

"Better," he murmured, before dipping his head down to hers.

His mouth grazed hers and he whispered against her lips.

"Kiss me," he said. "Show me how you like to be licked."

With a broken moan, she strained up and plunged her tongue into his mouth, before sliding it back out again to stroke his lips. He mimicked her movements, twirling his tongue with hers and matching each nip and suck she made.

She could taste herself on him. The thick flavor of her arousal on his tongue drove her crazy.

They kissed for what felt like hours, his hot dick pressing against her pulsing clit, their tongues dueling and twirling in an effort to tease and dominate.

When his hands trailed back up her torso and he lifted his head, she cried out in protest.

He gripped her shoulders and pushed her back against the seat, before pulling her skirt down to cover her legs.

"Time to go," he said.

She stared at him blankly for a moment before whipping her head to the side. Looking out the window, she saw that the limo had stopped in the curved driveway of the hotel.

Turning back to him, she watched as Lucas shrugged out of his jacket and draped it over his arm, no doubt to cover the large wet spot she'd made on the front of his pants.

She watched with growing frustration and appreciation as she realized that he'd planned his timing perfectly.

Despite her excruciating need for an orgasm, she couldn't help but compliment him.

"Damn. You're good," she said before releasing a soft chuckle.

He smiled as he helped her from the car.

"I know," he whispered back.

Eight

JESSICA STUMBLED FROM the limo and into the hotel.

Lucas held her elbow to his side and placed a hand at her back as he guided her through the lobby.

"Don't take this the wrong way, but I hate you so much right now," she whispered him.

"No offense taken," he said with a raspy laugh.

She teetered on her heels as they made their way down the long hall to the private elevator.

"Did you enjoy yourself tonight?" he asked as he pressed his code into the security pad.

"You know I did," she said, clenching her thighs tight in an attempt to relieve her throbbing sex.

The door slid open and he nudged her inside.

Before it closed shut behind them, he pushed her against the back wall and dropped to his knees.

She gasped when he shoved her dress up her hips and draped her right leg over his shoulder.

He slid his hands up her ass and canted her hips up—opening her to him further.

"What are you doing?" she asked, not caring for his answer so long as he continued making her burn.

"Claiming my goodnight kiss," he said before dipping his head forward and plunging his tongue through her folds.

Her legs buckled and he moaned against her pussy.

His hands gripped her tighter, holding her up and still for his devouring mouth.

She slammed one hand to the wall behind her and slid the other through his thick hair, holding his head tight to her sex.

He licked into her with deep, dragging strokes—his tongue plunging into her pussy before licking up her cunt and curling around her clit. She rode his face, rocking her hips in tune with his dancing tongue.

Yes!

A spiraling sensation coiled tight inside her, and she knew that she couldn't withstand one more stroke without exploding.

He tongue slowed, as if he sensed how close to climaxing she was. She shrieked out a protest, her senses past the need for teasing. She'd finally reached the edge of her control and her body begged for release, but Lucas held her still.

His plunged forward for another lingering taste before pulling her hand from his head and dropping her leg to the floor.

"No!" she said not ashamed to beg for more.

He stood and pressed the length of his body against hers.

Instead of pulling away as she'd thought, he gripped her ass and rubbed her against his erection. Eager for more she lifted her legs and wrapped her legs around his waist. He grunted his approval and bent his head down, capturing her mouth in a hot kiss.

She felt him shove away from the wall, but she was too lost in the fire of her need to pay attention to where he headed. Wrapping her arms around his neck she closed her eyes and held on tight, whimpering as each step he took rubbed his thick cock against her core.

She wanted to reach between them and grip him there—to slide her hands around his hardness and make him burn as much as she did, to put her mouth on him and taste his essence on her tongue.

Later, she promised herself.

Tonight, she wanted to feel him sink into her and stretch her wide. She wanted him to fill her up as he promised.

He pulled his lips away again, forcing her to open her eyes.

Looking around, she saw that he'd walked them to his room—the soft glow of his bed lamps lighting the space.

"Strip."

She didn't need him to repeat his husky demand—the need to feel him skin to skin was impossible to resist. Dropping her feet to the ground, she moaned at the drag of his hardness against her as she descended. He held her steady as she shoved off her shoes and reached to her side to slide the hidden zipper of her dress down. With one tug, the dress fell to the floor. With another quick flick of her wrists, her strapless bra joined it.

Lucas wasn't as quick to oblige with his clothing.

"Touch your breasts for me," he said as he loosened his tie.

She did as he said—reaching up to fondle her swollen breasts.

He pulled the tie over his head and tossed it over his shoulder. She watched as he unbuttoned his shirt slowly before shrugging it off. She licked her lips at every inch of skin exposed. His chest was as cut as she'd imagined— thick with sculpted muscles and sinew. He reached for his belt and she shifted her gaze down to the straining length tenting the front of his pants.

He kicked off his shoes and socks before he unsnapped his slacks and drew the zipper down. Underneath, he wore a pair of dark boxer briefs that hugged his solid thighs. When he hooked his hands in them, she stroked her fingers over her nipples and pinched them tight, anticipating his next move.

The boxers fell to the floor and she moaned at the meaty flesh revealed. His cock was long and thick; its girth proving Lucas didn't make idle promises.

She whimpered when he reached forward and gripped his cock. He shafted his length. His large hand stroking up and down. A drop of pre-cum glistened at the tip making her mouth water. Thoughts of sucking him deep into her mouth returned. She took a step forward holding out a hand to touch it but he stopped her with one word.

"No."

Her knees trembled at his denial, but she held still.

He walked to her, stopping with only leaving less than an inch of space between them. The hairs on his chest grazed her nipples and his hot length grazed her belly, making her gasp aloud and lean into him. He smoothed his hands up her arms, trailing his fingers over her shoulders and tunneling his hands in her thick hair.

Caressing his thumbs across her cheeks, he stared into her eyes.

"God you're beautiful," he said, his voice coming out in a gruff rasp.

She remained speechless in his grasp, her mind and body held rapt by the blazing heat and emotion she saw reflected in his eyes.

"This isn't a game anymore," he whispered.

The truth of his words washed over her, bringing tears to her eyes. Nothing they'd done all night truly felt like a game. Each encounter resulted in a discovery about herself and her feelings towards him. How could she have ever questioned whether he would be better than her fantasy? Her fantasy didn't make her hot like he did. Her fantasy didn't make her beg and burn the way Lucas could. The reality of being with him was much better than any fantasy or dream.

In that moment, she let her heart fill with the emotion she'd kept hidden for so long. She tucked that knowledge away, knowing the time to reveal her feelings would come soon, but tonight she wanted to lose herself in the heat they shared.

"It was never a game," she told him.

A look of triumph flickered over his face before he swept his mouth down for a deep kiss.

He walked her backward, and when the back of her knees hit the bed, she fell back, bouncing softly on the plush mattress. She scooted to the top of the bed and spread her legs wide. Lucas didn't waste any time crawling between them.

She hurried to wrap her legs around him, but his strong hands held her thighs down.

"Not yet," he said.

She groaned at the thought of any more foreplay. Her body couldn't stand another round of teasing.

Instead of making her wait, he reached to the nightstand, opened a condom and tossed her an evil grin.

She looked down to watch him put it on. He stroked the latex down his length, lingering to pump his shaft while she watched. Balanced on his knees between her legs, his cock straining towards her pussy—was the sexiest thing she'd ever seen. She tried again to move her legs, but Lucas was quick to hold her down.

"Do you remember what I told you tonight?" he asked.

I want to hold you wide open and see how long and hard I can fuck you until you scream my name.

Gyrating her hips beneath his hold, she answered him. "Yes."

"Good."

He gripped her thighs wide, tilting her cunt up to receive his hard length. His thumbs held her slick lips open, exposing her clit to them both. Shifting his hips, he worked his cock in slowly, sliding the big mushroom shaped tip inside and stopping.

She moaned at the stretch that one move made—her pussy straining to engulf him. Her core flooded with more moist heat—she could feel it dripping from her onto his shaft.

"So fucking sexy," her murmured, before pulling back and thrusting forward again.

He kept that maddening pace. Pulling back and thrusting forward, but only filling her with an inch at a time.

She wanted to close her eyes in agony, but she couldn't take her eyes away from his large cock working its way into her.

He plunged forward again, filling her with another delicious inch.

"Please," she begged, her breaths coming out in harsh pants.

"Not yet," he said.

He kept up that pace, adding another thick inch of his cock every few minutes. She got drunk on the sensation of him stretching her, but it wasn't enough. He withheld the last inch of his length from her, stroking into her with shallow thrusts, but never ramming her full.

Her pussy gushed around him, and her internal muscles throbbed and clenched wanting to pull him in deeper.

"Lucas…please!"

She wailed out the words, tears rolling from her eyes.

"Yes!" He hissed out the single word as he plunged forward, burying himself inside her to the hilt. She screamed his name again as he reared back and slammed into her again.

Gone was the slow leisurely pace he used to torture her— replaced with hard, deep thrusts slamming into her, riding her hard into a realm where nothing existed except his hot demands and his control of her body.

Harsh cries left her throat, as he rode her. She bucked beneath him, going wild—glorying in the hot blaze he stoked in her. The sound of her blood rushing filled her ears as her body coiled tight. He stroked his thumb over her clit, and she hurtled over the edge screaming as her orgasm claimed her.

The climax held her captive for long moments. Her body locked in a blazing fire as her pussy fluttered and tightened around his shaft.

She felt him stiffen above her and heard him moan deep as his cock pulsed inside her. He continued plunging into her with gentling strokes, before slowing to a stop and slumping down onto the bed beside her.

Speechless, she let him gather her close. She cuddled to his side wanting to stay wrapped in his warmth forever. Her mind drifted in a fog, as her exhausted body tugged her to sleep. Her last thought before drifting off was how she could have ever believed that she could walk away from Lucas.

Tomorrow, she promised herself. *Tomorrow.*

***

Lucas stretched awake, his mind coming slowly to awareness. Vivid images of the night before filled his head and he groaned as his body stirred awake.

Jessica.

Eyes closed, he stretched out a hand, feeling across the sheets for her warmth. He froze when his fingers touched nothing but air. Snapping open his eyes, he sat up. The space beside him was empty.

Swinging his legs to the floor, he hurried to the en-suite bathroom, but it was empty as well.

Shit.

He slumped against the doorjamb as the truth sank in.

She'd left.

He rubbed a hand against the cold ache spreading along his chest. He'd thought that they'd made a real connection last night, that he'd proven a relationship between them was worth a chance.

Had he really been that far off in reading the situation? Had she only wanted to indulge in a sexual experiment instead of exploring the possibility of anything deeper?

Shaking his head he didn't want to believe that he'd misjudged her feelings so wrongly.

I should have told her the truth.

He snorted at the thought. He could barely understand is feelings for her. How was he expected to explain to her that he'd fallen in love with her before even going on one date?

"Good Morning."

He whipped around at the husky voice behind him.

Jessica stood in the center of the room wearing his dress shirt from the night before. She looked at him—a soft smile playing across her lips.

"You're still here," he said in wonder.

Her smile dimmed and she took a step back. He thought he saw a flicker of hurt cross her features, but it disappeared quickly.

"I thought…"

She looked away as her voice trailed off and cleared her throat.

"It doesn't matter. I'll go get my things," she said, turning to walk away.

"No!" he shouted.

He hurried over to her, blocking her path.

"That's not what I meant."

She looked at him in confusion.

"I thought that you'd left—that you'd decided last night was a mistake."

Relief flashed across her face as she shook her head.

"No, I just wanted to order breakfast, but I didn't want to wake you," she said.

He grabbed her hand and grinned down at her.

"So you've decided to stay?" he asked.

She nodded and smiled back at him.

"Yes," she said

He let out a loud whoop and pulled her to his chest, lifting her off the ground.

She hugged him tight as he whirled her around, her soft curves fitting perfectly against his chest. His cock began to harden and he groaned. Slowing to a stop, he set her down.

He didn't want his libido to hijack his chance at letting Jessica know how he felt.

Cupping her face in his hands, he looked into her warm eyes and took the plunge.

"I know this is going to sound a little strange but I think I'm a little in love with you," he said.

She frowned up at him.

"What did I tell you about your lack of finesse," she asked.

"Jessica I—"

"For someone who's read so much psychology you suck in the romance department," she continued.

His heart sank when she pulled away.

"Let me show you how it's done," she said.

The lines on her face softened as she rose on her tiptoes, cupped his face and stared deep into his eyes.

"Lucas, I fell in lust with you in my fantasies and fell in love with you in real life. It doesn't matter if our first date was last night or last year. Somewhere along the line, I fell in love with you and I don't care how or when it happened. Only that I get the chance to do it over and over again."

His pulse raced as her words set in.

"You see that wasn't so hard was it?" she said.

He wrapped his arms around her and pulled her tight.

"You took the words right out of my mouth," he whispered against her lips before sealing them with a searing kiss.

The End

Dear Reader,

Thank you so much for taking the time to read *Rapt*. I hope you enjoyed the read. If so, I also hope you find the time to leave a review and let me know what you think.

If you'd like to learn more about other books I've written, visit my website. And if you'd like to be notified of any of my new books or events, sign-up for my author newsletter here, to get an email notification on release day.

Happy reading!

Laurel
www.laurelcremant.com
@LaurelCremant

Other Books by Laurel Cremant

Erotic Contemporary

Negotiating Skills
Persuasion Skills
Rapt (An Erotic Tale)

Paranormal/Fantasy

Midnight Mistletoe (The Golden Pack Alphas: Book I)
Midnight Dare (The Golden Pack Alphas: Book II)
Midnight Truce (The Golden Pack Alphas: Book III)
Midnight Guard (The Golden Pack Alphas: Book IV)
Midnight Born (The Golden Pack Alphas: Book V)
Golden Pack Alphas (The Complete Series)
Wynter's Fall (Wynter Tales: Book I)

About the Author

Laurel is a romance author, who like most writers loves to read. She has no one favorite because she believes *"a good story is a good story"* regardless of what genre. However, her first love (pun intended) is romance. From the sappy YA romance novel to the more risqué erotica novels, Laurel is a sucker for a good love story.

Laurel writes paranormal and contemporary romance and is a self-proclaimed, out of the closet nerd. She admits that she can't seem to avoid adding a bit of "nerdology" or "geek-dom" to all of her books. Living in Miami, she also admits that she can't seem to avoid giving her heroines gorgeous shoes, *"In Miami, we worship everything strappy, open toed and just plain hot!"*

Visit Laurel at www.LaurelCremant.com to learn more about her new and upcoming releases. You can also contact Laurel across the internet via email (laurelcremant@gmail.com), Twitter (@LaurelCremant) and Facebook (LaurelCremantAuthor).

More steamy romance by Laurel Cremant now available
at most major book retailers

PERSUASION SKILLS

MIDNIGHT MISTLETOE

WYNTER'S FALL

Read on for a sneak peek…

Persuasion Skills

A Contemporary Romance

In the aftermath of a major health scare, Pepper Holts makes the relief-inspired decision to seize the day. Unfortunately, most of her "seizing" involves a bit of merlot and her best friend's pants! After a shared night of passion she realizes that her feelings for Jax are a lot more complicated than she ever thought.

Jax has finally realized that his allergy to marriage has nothing to do with the institution itself, and everything to do with the women in his bed—or more specifically, the one woman not in his bed. Her reaction to their one night together has him scrambling to regroup. So he does what he knows best—he disappears, and he thinks. The plan?—convince Pepper into staying with him at a secluded cabin for one week. One week of pretending to be a happily married couple to show her how great they could be together.

One

This is where dragons be.

THE SILLY PHRASE from spontaneous childhood road trips with her family flickered through Pepper's mind as she drove along a jagged dirt road. One no doubt built to destroy a car's suspension and bruise a passenger's ass. As a matter of fact, calling the bumpy, rocky path a road was a kindness.

Gritting her teeth, she gripped the steering wheel harder as she drove through yet another deep rut and bounced roughly in the driver's seat. No amount of expensive soft leather seating was enough to protect her rear end from hurting.

She mentally catalogued every bounce and responding bruise, adding them to Jaxon Grey's list of sins. She growled softly as the anger she'd kept leashed all morning came rushing back to the surface. He was the reason she was driving through the cold Colorado Mountains instead of being in the warm, welcoming climate back home in Miami.

Her ever-reclusive, volatile business partner, and fast approaching former best friend, had been missing in action for several weeks, and she was long past exhausted from holding down the fort without him.

Together, they both owned equal shares of their company eTheorial Inc., a research and development firm specializing in electronics.

She smacked her hand against the steering wheel in frustration. Like Jax was handling his fifty percent at the moment. He was *handling* diddly squat! He'd left her high and dry to take care of it all.

They'd met in college and became fast friends while she majored in business and he focused on both computer and electrical engineering. When they had started the company, the joke was that she was the brains and he was the talent. They made a great team, and the company had grown and prospered over the last few years through blood, sweat, and tears. He went about creating magic in the lab, and she slew dragons in the boardroom.

Snorting loudly, she slowed the car down to search for the "slight right" the GPS insisted was up ahead.

"I didn't sign up to play Indiana Jones," she mumbled. Spotting the turn, she let out a groan. This new road seemed in even worse condition.

"The things I do for the company." She sighed and shook her head before maneuvering onto the path. Thinking of how hard they had both worked to make eT a success only made her more determined to drag him back to Miami one way or another. The phrase *dead or alive* flashed through her mind after she hit a particularly deep pot hole.

Sadly, the poor condition of the road made her feel better about her decision the week before to postpone her trip up the mountains.

She'd originally planned to make the drive eight days prior. Unfortunately, Mother Nature had seen fit to start the snow season early that year, effectively delaying her plans for several days.

She continued to bob by endless rows of snow-tipped trees and bit back a curse. Basic common sense and logic proved that he wasn't responsible for the weather, but she was adding it to his list of transgressions anyway.

As much as she wanted to physically maim Jax and drag him home, she wasn't crazy enough to drive along unfamiliar mountain roads through the snow. No way was she going to become the basis for some *Lifetime* Movie Of The Week.

So she'd bided her time and waited for both the weather and road conditions to clear before setting out on her trip.

She gritted her teeth at the soreness seeping into her rear end.

Under normal circumstances, she would have hired a driver familiar with the area. A small part of her brain also worried about anyone else witnessing just how upset she was with her reclusive partner, so she didn't want anyone around when she finally confronted Jax.

Her lips tightened as she thought about the last set of text messages they'd exchanged.

He'd postponed yet another important meeting with the company's lawyers to discuss the finalization of the purchase of Lubtech, an up and coming software firm. A takeover that she'd spent the last year and a half working hard to make happen. Without Jax present, she couldn't move forward, and he refused to give her his proxy.

He-Man: Hey Pep, can't make the Lubtech meeting. Reschedule.
Me: We can't postpone again. Get down to Miami ASAP!
He-Man: No can do.
Me: Then give me your proxy. I will handle on my end.
He-Man: No
Me: Stop being an ASS!
He-Man: Stop being a BRAT! See you in a few weeks.

That last text had caused her to throw her phone across the room, smashing it against the opposite wall. The device splintered and shattered into small electronic pieces, giving her a split second of satisfaction before she added its demise to Jaxon's list of wrongdoings. It was the third phone she'd destroyed since he decided to pull his disappearing act.

As she'd stared at the shiny broken parts scattered on the floor across the room, she'd made the decision to come looking for him.

She'd already tried previously to get the manifests from their corporate jet, but Jax had somehow managed to bribe the flight crew from telling her anything. When she approached their VP of Research and Development, the woman had only blinked owlishly at her and said that Jax phoned her twice a day to make sure everything was running smoothly in the labs. Outside of that, the woman knew nothing of his whereabouts.

After a few more fruitless conversations with staff and a short phone call to his sister, she had no choice but to lure his ever-efficient assistant away from his desk long enough to search for Jax's latest billing statements. He was notorious for liking the finer things in life even before their success with eT, so wherever he chose to hide out, he would leave an extensive money trail.

After some quick spying, she'd been surprised to see that there had been only one major charge to his credit cards in the last three months — a cabin rental in somewhere named Lissit, Colorado. When she'd investigated further, she'd learned that Jax had rented the cabin through the remainder of the year. The news had only fueled her anger. No way was she waiting another two months for him to decide to return to Miami.

Thinking of that blaze of anger made her stomach burn with acid. The ensuing rush hadn't helped matters, either. She was on the plane to Colorado within twenty-four hours. When she'd arrived, she'd taken the time to buy a satellite phone, some warm clothing, and rent an SUV equipped for trekking through the mountains.

The weather delay had only served to increase her frustration. She had a lot of work still left to do regarding the acquisition of Lubtech, and there was only so much she could get done from her laptop within her hotel room.

It also gave her too much free time to think about Jax and the state of their relationship.

She ran a hand over her face and shook her head in confusion.

After years of friendship, she couldn't believe that Jax would just up and abandon her when he knew how hard she had worked to secure the deal. She just didn't understand his behavior lately. They had been friends throughout college and had survived financial ups and downs, family tragedies, and recent health issues together.

Her mind skittered away from the memory of the breast cancer scare she'd had three months earlier. She touched her chest, an unconscious gesture to reassure herself she was still okay.

Jaxon had been her rock through the whole thing. He was the first person she had run to when she noticed something odd in her left breast, and he was the one who sat with her, gripping her hand in support, when she was told the cyst was benign.

She could feel a flush work its way up her throat as she thought of that day. Relief had crashed through at her results, and she was lucky to have been given a clean bill of health. However, she still remembered that day with a profound sense of embarrassment. *If only I had avoided that last glass of wine.*

Perhaps if she hadn't had that last glass of liquid courage, her relationship with Jax wouldn't be so awkward right now.

The car ran into another pothole, and she cursed under her breath. At the jolt, or at the memory of that night? She nibbled on her lower lip, not wanting to know the answer.

She'd always had a bit of a crush on him, ever since he had shown up in the middle of a dicey situation she'd gotten into in college. Over the years, she'd excused her infatuation based on the fact that Jax was an incredibly handsome man, and a woman would have to be blind, deaf, dumb, and possibly an extra terrestrial not to appreciate his good looks. But even the aliens would at least look twice.

The only indication of his Italian roots could be seen in the smooth olive tint to his skin. With his broad shoulders and tall frame, he'd always reminded her a bit of a super-hero, right down to his wavy honey-blond hair that always managed to fall over his intense dark-green eyes and the damn dimple that constantly seemed to wink at her when he smiled.

She caught herself smiling softly at the thought of those sexy dimples and scowled.

He completely negated the skinny nerd stereotype, which just made his sexy quotient tick up even higher. A sexy meathead Pepper could appreciate then ignore, but a hunky genius? *Not a chance.*

Perhaps it had always been inevitable that she would make a fool of herself with him eventually. And of course, with her luck, it wasn't him catching her staring at his butt for the millionth time, or noticing how her nipples tended to tighten up whenever he entered a room.

Nope.

Those scenarios would have been preferable. Instead, she had to make the merlot-inspired decision to strip in front of him and beg him to make love to her.

Shifting uncomfortably in the leather seat, Pepper replayed that day, more specifically that night, over in her mind for what must have been the millionth time.

Jax, as usual, had been an amazing friend. Just as she had been there for him only a few months prior when his mother passed away, he'd dropped everything to help her through the doctor's visits, biopsy, and ultimate good news that the lump she found was nothing serious.

After the last appointment, he had taken her out to dinner to celebrate, and the night should have ended at that. Unfortunately, Pepper was so relieved she was healthy that she made the drunken decision to finally act on her long-standing attraction to Jax.

The giddy need to seize life and finally live out her fantasy had almost ruined their relationship. For one night, she'd let herself live out what she had only allowed herself to imagine for years. Even now, the event caused her panties to go damp and her body to prickle with heat.

"Do you trust me, Pep?"

The huskily asked words whispered through her mind.

She had always known Jax was an intensely focused man, but to have all of that raw energy concentrated on her was one of the most erotic things she'd ever experienced.

The idea of allowing someone else to control her pleasure had always appealed to her, but she'd never trusted anyone enough to give them that power. But with Jax ... with him, she had relinquished everything.

"Yes."

She whimpered softly into the cabin of the plush rental car as her body heated, remembering the feel of him rubbing against her flesh, his hard chest pressing against her nipples as he pulled her hands above the bed and tied them loosely to the headboard.

She remembered the sense of freedom when she gripped the edges of his silk tie bond around her wrists.

"That's it, honey. Let me in."

A shiver worked its way down her spine as her body relived the memory of his almost bruising grip holding her hips down as he kneeled between her legs, circling his cock at her wet entrance.

The sound of his hisses of breath and grunts of satisfaction. The pressure of his lips against hers. The slow licks of tongue and soft nips of teeth. The force of his hard length slowly working its way into her was ingrained in her memory forever.

If only it hadn't been the worst mistake of her life.

Sadly, that night had forced her to recognize that she felt more than just attraction for Jax. Finally sleeping with him forced her to see that her love for him went way past the confines of friendship and into something more. Pepper had woken up that morning realizing she was in love with her best friend and had been for years, and it terrified her.

She had heard that morning-afters could be awkward, but nothing had prepared her for the feeling of sheer panic and terror that had gripped her when she woke to find him looking at her with a look of regret hovering on his face.

She'd had Jaxon in her arms and bed, but the cold light of day had shown that he'd only stayed to spare her from embarrassment.

Sputtered excuses of too much alcohol and the promise that they should both forget the whole thing had ever happened had quickly fallen from her lips as she'd ushered him out of her bed and home.

The burn of that shame engulfed her, and she powered the heater off hoping the return of cold air in the cabin would help her to escape that humiliating feeling.

There had been a few stilted conversations and awkward moments after that, but their years of friendship had persevered. At least, that's what she'd initially believed.

Just as Pepper had finally thought they were beginning to feel comfortable with each other again, he'd surprised her by stating he would be taking a few weeks off, and he had been virtually incommunicado ever since.

Another jarring dip brought her back to the present. She focused back on the road and glanced at her navigation display, thankful she hadn't missed her turnoff. According to the little screen, she was less than an hour away from the cabin Jax had rented.

Her pulse quickened, as it always did at the thought of seeing him, but the excitement was quickly doused by the simmering anger that had burned in her ever since he left her.

Midnight Mistletoe

A Paranormal Romance
Book I of the Golden Pack Alphas Series

All were-hybrid, Georgia Walker wants for Christmas is to spend some time away from her pack and in particular, away from one increasingly dangerous enforcer turned Beta. She has every intention of spending her days basking in the warm Caribbean sun and indulging in an island fling, or two. Anything to forget the way a certain were made her pulse race and skin tingle.

Marcus Legrand has only one goal this holiday season, bring Georgia home and finally claim her for his own. Convincing the strong willed ice princess will take all of his skill and patience, but Marcus is no stranger to hunting prey. He has every intention of putting both his rank and heart on the line.

One

Prey always made the same mistake—they ran.

STANDING MOTIONLESS AT the floor to ceiling windows of his hotel room, Marcus Legrand looked out at the umbrella dotted beach beyond. He savored the weight of anticipation and awareness that had cloaked him ever since he'd learned that Gigi had run—again.

A smile twitched his lips. She would never admit that, nor would she appreciate his use of the pet name he'd assigned to her. Strong willed and stubborn Georgia Walker never ran from anyone or anything—except him.

From the moment he'd first visited her pack, the prickly woman loved to avoid and drive him crazy in equal measure.

As a High Council *Maat*, an enforcer of the laws and rites agreed upon hundreds of years ago by the original wolf packs, he preferred his life well ordered. He knew all too well the chaos and destruction that came with flaunting pack rules.

He was that chaos. He was that destruction.

Gigi didn't seem to care. She was out there on the beach. No doubt celebrating her supposed coup in evading him.

It always amused Marcus how easily a person underestimated a *were*—specifically a werewolf—specifically *him*. But Gigi should have known better. As the daughter to Darius, the Golden Pack alpha she was more than privy to Council politics and the foolishness in taunting him, and yet she did it anyway.

Her willingness to pick a fight stirred more than just the wolf in him—it woke the man. It had been a long time since any woman, shifter or otherwise aroused any interest in him. Even longer since one did more than make his cock twitch in interest. But from the moment he saw her and inhaled her heady scent, he'd wanted nothing more than to throw her over his shoulder and steal her away.

He'd been overwhelmed with that urge, and even now, after a year to come to terms with what it all meant, he struggled to tamp down on the compulsion to drag her to the nearest surface and fuck her until they both passed out into oblivion.

I have to catch her first.

Marcus gave a mental shrug. For him, the hunt was always the easy part. He reached up and ran his left hand along his opposite arm. Although, covered by the thin layer of his shirt, he traced the fine lines of the tattoos beneath. Every one as firmly etched in his memory as on his skin.

Each symbolizing a kill or judgment made. They were reminders of what he was and the role he'd chosen to play.

As a lone wolf, the Council had recruited him years ago—more years than most knew. They'd taken him in, shielded his true origins and in return he'd become their hammer. The one they called upon to meet out justice. He'd never regretted his choice.

He understood the necessity of having a feared weapon on your side when approaching the bargaining table. Fear often created the best compromise. When the Council called upon his services it signaled the end of negotiations.

He'd become accustomed to people watching him with unease and deference. Even the few women he engaged with, were more interested in the thrill of sleeping with an enforcer, than anything else. Yet Georgia's eyes contained a different look entirely.

Her deep brown eyes challenged and aroused with each look, each raise of the brow and each drop of eyelash.

Thinking back on the cool reception she'd given him when he'd first arrived in Golden Valley a year ago, the sadistic part of him smiled at his choice of conquest. Unlike other women, Gigi was not in awe of him. She didn't hold her tongue or pretend meekness. Her countenance screamed alpha, and had his wolf—and another part of his anatomy, standing up to take notice from the start.

She'd stood at her father's side, tall and proud, her long dark hair falling around her shoulders in waves, framing toffee skin and high rounded cheek bones. Her plush mouth firmed in disdain and she quirked one delicate eyebrow at him.

"Oh goodie, the new pit bull is here."

Her husky voice delivered the cutting words without a single waver or pause. He'd noted it as possibly the sexiest thing he'd ever heard.

At first he'd believed his reaction stemmed from her heat cycle. He could smell it on her—the thick musk of her arousal swirling through his senses, almost drowning him in the need to slant her stubborn chin up and sink his teeth into the succulent flesh of her neck.

Despite her obvious initial dislike of him, her eyes had flared with an answering blaze of attraction.

Meeting her tilted his whole world off its axis and he knew things would never be the same.

Whether she chose to admit it, they'd both chosen at that moment to withdraw to their respective corners. He'd come to the valley on official orders from the Council and had no time for small dalliances or otherwise. Whatever reasons she had for retreating remained her own.

He'd been sent to help deal with a rogue pack. Gigi's father, not wanting to endanger his own people, had called upon the Council to help deal with the matter. Rogue wolves were dangerous on several levels. Not only did they refuse to obey the rules set in place to protect *weres* from discovery, they had no respect for life, human or otherwise.

Under normal circumstances, the Council would not have stepped in. Most rogue packs, died a natural death. The absence of no true alpha in the group always led to them killing each other off in a useless quest to dominate. But this pack had been different. Not only were they deliberately breaking the rules, they'd begun kidnapping humans and turning them. That, the Council could not ignore.

Dealing with them hadn't taken much time. But there had been some casualties, one of them being Darius' Beta. In the end the group had been defeated and dispatched. Justice was met and his job was done—seven new feathers added to his collection. However during his stay, he'd developed an attachment to the Golden Pack that was... unexpected.

After delivering his report to the Council, Marcus had returned to Golden Valley—and to Gigi.

As an enforcer he had the right to set up base where ever he chose, and for the time being, he'd settled on the biting cold mountains of Golden Valley. He'd even agreed to play temporary beta to Darius.

He liked the pushy alpha. His twinkling eyes, booming voice and ready smile were too easily misconstrued as trusting and easy-going, but Marcus had seen him in battle. Darius was one of the shrewdest wolves he'd ever encountered—and deadliest. Traits he had no doubt passed down to his only daughter.

The dynamic between Darius and the other wolves intrigued him.

None in the group resented their alpha's choice in mate, Genevieve, Gigi's mother. Her being a witch didn't seem to bother the other wolves. Yet for some he'd seen that an obvious weariness of Gigi herself existed.

Her hybrid status put them on edge. A part of them questioned her right to belong. In that he could sympathize with her. He understood the difficulties of being different in a world that expected sameness.

It was strange to him—being surrounded by a collective. The feeling wasn't entirely bad, just different.

He'd never given any consideration to becoming part of any one pack. Both his history and need for privacy didn't lend themselves to community living.

Yet he'd stayed. He set up house in a small bungalow close to Darius's large home. He'd chosen the location in small part to be available to Darius and in larger part to be near Gigi—her cottage only a few yards on the other side of the main house. Each day he grew more attached to the land and each day wanted Gigi with a need that bordered on obsession.

She avoided him—evaded his presence with a skill he had to admire. He reveled in their power struggle.

Just before her recent disappearing act, he'd found her leaving her father's office, back straight and eyes flashing.

"Bad day?"

"Fuck off."

"Such a lady."

"And you're such a pest."

He reached out and touched her arm, pausing her marching progression.

"In a suicidal mood today?"

"With you? Always. Now tell me what has you so upset."

Her nostrils flared and she leaned into him.

"You. You bother me. When are you going to saddle up and find yourself a new pack to annoy?"

"Maybe as soon as you stop running."

Her lips curled up in a sneer.

"I don't run from anyone Legrand. If I choose to not be around you it means that I see no need in spending time with arrogant pricks."

He stroked a hand up her waist and brushed a fingertip over one tight nipple.

"And yet, those sensitive nipples of yours say differently every time I see you."

She returned the favor, running a hand down his front and cupped his hard cock.

"And your dick seems to have the same problem," she said, her voice almost sickly sweet.

Their gazes held as he pinched her nipple, and she squeezed his shaft.

"It would be a shame for you if I had to rip it off," she whispered before wrenching away from his hold and storming away.

He'd watched her walk away with a smile on his face. Even the threat of dismemberment hadn't been enough for his arousal to subside. He considered each encounter with her as progress. Soon, she would admit that there was more between them than just simple attraction.

Focusing back on the beach, he narrowed his gaze a specific pink umbrella poised haphazardly in the sand.

He touched a hand to his suit pocket, feeling at the note folded inside. Darius, had requested, that he bring Gigi home for Christmas. But even if Darius hadn't asked him to find Gigi, Marcus would have come for her. They'd spent the last year tiptoeing around each other, and it had to stop.

Dropping his hands down to his sides he turned from the window and strode to the door. It was time to go hunting.

Wynter's Fall

A Modern Contemporary Fairy Tale
Book 1 of the Wynter Tales series

An unsuspecting mortal, A Keeper of Dreams, And a group of Gods intent on reclaiming powers they no longer deserve...

Melania Wynter has a big problem, the man of her actual dreams is becoming all too real. Determined to gain back some control over her life, she hopes that a a little vacation will be enough for her psyche to stop comparing her real life to the vivid dreams she's had since childhood. But one patch of ice, a solid pine tree and a nasty bump on the head derail her plans.

Daimone, Keeper of Dreams has always been drawn to Melania. He's bided his time, waiting for her to cross-over to his realm, but manipulative God's have interfered in unexpected ways. With a helping hand from fate, he must go to Melania and keep her safe.

Together they must navigate the wilderness and survive both the cold and trouble-making Gods.

One

*P*EOPLE LIED.

You don't see your whole life flash before your eyes when you die. You only saw white—blinding, unforgiving white.

No one also said that your last moments would have a soundtrack of Adele's Skyfall *punctuated by the thudding of your heart and squealing tires.*

Gripping the steering wheel tight, Melania Wynter stared through the windshield of her spinning car, her throat frozen with fear as the world whirled around her.

Her pulse hammered in her ears as she pounded her foot on the brake pedal, hoping to stop the vehicle from its spiraling journey across the icy dark road.

She knew the moment the car left the asphalt; a sudden moment of harsh, crunching noise as the wheels hit slick gravel. But before they could gain any traction, the SUV completed another dizzying turn.

Her perception slowed down to microseconds of time accentuated by exploding pain. The seat belt tightened, pulling her shoulders and abdomen backwards in a bone-jarring jerk. The piercing sound of crushing metal pierced her ears in a mind numbing screech just before a white fist hurtled towards her face and everything faded to darkness.

***

Something is wrong.

Daimone stood frozen in the hall just outside of the Library of Dreams. His muscles locked and his long wings drew up and pinched closed at his shoulder blades as an icy tendril of foreboding slithered down his back. The scent of cinnamon wafted through the air and quickly disappeared. Its spicy aroma flared pungent for a quick moment before dying out into a stale shadow.

Melania.

Clenching his fists at his sides, he closed his eyes and cast his mind out, reaching for their mental bond. His heart sped as he examined the bright red thread that linked her to him. At first glimpse, he noticed nothing unusual; as usual, it burned bright, swirling like a crimson ribbon through the net of strings connecting him to other latents. He held his breath as he followed it farther across the plane.

His heart ceased when he encountered the frayed edges. Despite its brightness, the cord seemed to be almost wilting.

He'd seen patterns like this a million times. Experience told him it meant only one thing, but his mind refused to acknowledge the damning evidence.

It's too soon.

Reaching further with his mind, he followed the link, pushing at Melania's mind. Relief rushed through him when she opened for him, but the swirl of pink and blue mist he associated with her psyche at rest didn't appear. Instead, he stood surrounded by a cloud of dark gray.

"Melania, love?"

He furrowed his brow at the silence that greeted him. As Keeper of Dreams, he never had problems working his way into a person's mind. Especially not latents like Melania.

Something about her had always drawn him to her. When he'd first encountered her and saw her manipulate a dream to her liking, he knew she possessed the strongest untrained power he'd ever dealt with.

One of his jobs as a Keeper entailed that he trained and mentored gifted latents under his domain when they matured. Latents destined to cross over to his command became *somniaes*—soldiers and protectors of dreams.

He connected to most latents only in a dream state, but things had always been different with Melania. From the beginning, he'd reached her waking or asleep. In her childhood, he visited with her in his physical form, testing her talent and skills as a potential *somniae*. But as she grew older, he restricted their time together to only the dream realm. He'd worried that the Gods, always looking for a weak moment, might notice his fascination. In dreams, he would be aware of any unwanted scrutiny.

The first time he'd followed the crimson rope to her mind, she'd only been a child. When he'd entered her dream, he'd found her, barely a toddler, playing in a field of flowers.

She wore a white frilly dress, bunched around her in frothy disarray as she sat on the grass. Dark, baby-fine hair curled around her head—wisps of it caressing her chubby, cinnamon-colored cheeks.

She'd surrounded herself with large, life-like renditions of toys and stuffed animals. They were playing with her, chattering nonsense as she giggled.

A plump, purple unicorn trotted around her, its long pink mane sparkling in the sun. Clapping her hands, Melania chortled as the creature flicked its tail to the tinkling melody drifting in the air.

Two fluffy blue teddy bears sat around her with small plates of cookies and sweets in a cheerful rainbow of colors. Reaching forward with her small hands, she'd captured a sprinkle-bedecked cupcake and buried her mouth into it.

The scene had made him smile. For a child so young, she'd created such a vivid scene he knew then that she had the potential of being a powerful *somniae* one day. But what happened next confirmed his suspicions even more.

He stayed for a few minutes, intrigued by the small tug at his chest whenever he looked her. He felt protective of her from the moment he saw her and instead of fighting the connection, he chose to analyze it instead.

Unaware of his perusal and, due to her age, she lacked the communication skills for him to ask any questions. About to leave her to her dream land, the tell-tale signs of two *oneiros* advancing encroached on his perception.

The vivid Technicolor world she'd created dimmed. Not a dramatic change; only a slight greying in shade as if a thin cloud drifted over the sun.

As the Keeper of Dreams, more than familiar with the spirits that caused nightmares, their presence made him curious. The dreams of children were seldom worth the bother of one *oneiro*, let alone two. They tended to visit older youths capable of producing more expressive and lucid landscapes.

Every being exuded a unique frequency. Some may call them auras, but regardless of their names, certain casts reverberated an energy that became more pronounced in dream state. *Oneiro* tended toward the low bass-like tones on the spectrum.

Their presence always brought an ominous strumming. Most people remained consciously aware of it, but there was always a moment in dreams, just before a nightmare began, when a person knew something was out of place. An *oneiro* presence defined that moment. Masking his whereabouts, he observed their arrival.

The *oneiros* weren't evil creatures; they were just doing what they were born to do—cast nightmares. Daimone understood that where some dreams brought solace and escape, nightmares often brought clarity.

Although Daimone had control over his own forces, the *somniaes*, he had little control of the nightmare spirits. They were unpredictable at best, downright terrifying at worst. As long as they weren't being malicious, he let them be. Only rarely did he ever force one out of someone's dreams.

They entered Melania's dreamscape in a swirl of grey and black, withering the field of flowers around them.

Their wings shone bright in the deceptive pure white of their kind, the quills glittering like silver. Melania had stared at them as they smiled down at her.

That had been a first for Daimone. In all of the eternities he'd served as a Keeper, he had never witnessed an *oneiro* smile—unless a smile to elicit terror. Yet, the grins he saw had no malicious intent.

They began to change her dream, transforming her dancing toys to ugly, cackling versions of their former selves.

Melania's eyes had grown wide at the change, her mouth hanging open in what Daimone assumed to be the beginning of a scared wail.

Shock sliced through him when a chortle escaped instead.

She'd *laughed*—a huge grin spreading across her young cherub face as she stumbled up and began marching alongside the new, manic-looking toys, clapping happily.

After some time, she even began to enhance the nightmare the *oneiro* created, making the animals grow bigger and more imposing.

The pony sprouted long dark wings, the long locks of its mane twisting into hissing snakes. The once adorable bears grew claws and fangs, roaring into the darkened sky.

They embodied terror and a strange beauty all at once.

The *oneiros* exchanged a brief nod before disappearing as quickly as they appeared, leaving behind a happy Melania and a puzzled Daimone.

As the years passed, Daimone continued visiting Melania in her dreams, changing his appearance as she aged and masking his presence completely when *oneiros* visited her.

The protectiveness he felt for her since that first encounter only grew stronger. He'd stayed away for several years in her youth, when it looked as if her affection towards him had grown into attraction. Until then, he'd never given a thought to the fact that her childhood had quickly passed by.

She'd only been a teenager then and he still remembered the triumphant look in her eyes when she'd stolen a kiss. Surprised at both her actions and his reaction to her chaste peck, he'd left. But he didn't leave her completely; he still kept tabs on her—the compulsion to observe her never waned. He didn't approach her in her dreams for a long time, preferring to stay hidden within the fantastic worlds she built when she slept.

Many years later would he feel an undeniable urge to approach her again.

He found her weeping on a solitary bench. She had no dream world constructed around her, just a dark blue mist. He'd studied her face, noting how her curling tufts of hair had grown into a long mop just as unruly. How her dark skin, although still smooth, had shifted to accommodate high cheekbones, large green eyes with a slight tilt to them, and a mouth set in a perpetual kiss. Being near her—seeing her grown into womanhood—had been like a punch to his plexus.

When she glanced up at him with her tear-stained face, his heart had constricted.

"They're dead," she said. "Mom and Dad are gone."

He'd sat down next to her, draped his arm over her shoulders, and cocooned her to his side. She'd snuggled in deep, her tears wrenching at his heart. In that moment, he'd known he wouldn't ever be able to walk away from her again. Because despite her pain, the moment he pulled her into his arms, Daimone felt as if a missing puzzle piece had finally fallen into place.

The strong urge to protect her remained but somehow, somewhere through the years, he'd fallen in love with the girl who played with nightmares.

As she mourned her lost parents, he lamented the twisted humor of the gods.

As a Keeper, his world contained too much danger. The Gods were always playing games, and they wouldn't hesitate to use her as a pawn to control him. Love, and all of its myriad enticements, was not part of his destiny, but he would no longer deny his need to see Melania.

His decision made, he pulled her tighter to his side. He let her cry with no admonishment, offering her the comfort she needed and closeness he realized he craved.

Concentrating now, he pushed deeper into her mind and slowly, the mist cleared. He found her hovering bare in the ether of darkness. She floated—her long, dark limbs hanging loose and lank. She appeared to be sleeping, much like those fairytale princesses from the stories he used to tell her as a child.

He studied her face for any signs of pain or distress, but her features remained soft, at rest. The jaw so steadfastly set at a stubborn tilt lay relaxed and the plush lips that constantly tempted him formed a soft pout.

Her long, curling hair hung heavy like a curtain in the air beneath her. He let his gaze drift down her body, taking in the dips and curves that never failed to arouse appreciation.

But her sleeping state made no sense. Something had to be wrong, to force her mind into a state of internal sleep.

Placing a palm over her chest, he felt the faint flutter of her heart. The delicate thumping calmed him a bit as he pushed harder against her mind, flashes of memory began to filter out. They played through his brain as if they were his own and confirmed the reason behind her current unconscious state.

The stiffness in his shoulders loosened. She still lived, but most likely had injuries.

Opening his eyes, he reached forward and wrenched open the doors of the library.

He strode ahead, his wings snapping open and out around him, not bothering to acknowledge anyone he who crossed his path. Their loud gasps and startled expressions barely registered as he made his way across the long room, keeping his gaze focused on the floor-to-ceiling display of hourglasses at the end of the room.

Reaching the wall, he let his gaze glide up before settling on his objective.

Three hundred and thirty-third to the right. Four hundred and twentieth up. He knew each location of his latents by heart, but the one belonging to Melania had always drawn him. From the moment the fates had placed it on his shelves, he'd felt its hum.

Not bothering to turn his head to address his staff, he barked out an order.

"Leave!"

The snap of his wings as he dipped low and cast himself up drowned out the rustling of departing feet. He flew up to the high center of the wall and stared fixedly at the clear glass bulbs.

Each hourglass in the case represented the life span of a latent. The swirling sands drifted from the top orbs to the bottom at different speeds, completely dependent on the latents' specified time of cross-over.

Thousands of people were born latents, but the honor of crossing over and becoming a *somniae* required more than just latent talent.

Destiny proved a tricky combination of fate and free will. Each latent came into the world with a mark, stamping the number of years they were meant to experience life on Earth. For those latents who died before the time embedded on their flesh, they went on to whatever afterlife their actions had destined them to.

However, making it to their predetermined age didn't necessarily mean they were automatically welcomed into the ranks of the *somniae*. They still had the daunting task of proving to the fates that they'd earned the destiny they'd been cut. That's where free will came into play.

The choices each latent made throughout their lives ultimately decided if they would become *somniae*, the dream walkers. They were trained to guard and protect dreams from malicious attacks and manipulations by the gods.

The task was far from easy.

Eons ago during the God Wars, many gods misused their ability to control *pranx*, the three sacred realms—dreams, fate, and justice. They manipulated them for their own gain in the hopes of defeating each other. The founding Gods stood aside in the beginning, wanting their children to settle their differences alone. But when Petra, the daughter of Death, manipulated fate and killed her brother, they had no choice but to step in.

In the aftermath, the founders, disgusted and saddened over the carnage their children had caused, gathered together and decided that a parliament of guardians would be formed. Each founder chose one trusted soldier from their legion and, banding together, they fused their powers and essence together to form the Keepers.

Their union stripped the remaining gods of all control of the *pranx*, imbuing those powers to the newly formed Keepers. Although the Gods no longer had control over the realms, they still had access and many still actively breached the rules in the hopes of regaining their old control.

As the captain of Janax, the Sky God's guard, Daimone became the Guardian and Keeper of dreams. He trained *somniaes,* dream weavers, when they were sent into the hall—their main objective to prevent the gods from ever using the *pranx* for wrongdoing again.

Before Melania, he watched over the latents and checked in on them occasionally, but he focused most of his time training those who crossed over and became *somniaes*. Between training and avoiding becoming part of the political games the other gods enjoyed playing, he didn't spare much time for anyone—except her.

Melania had always been special. She'd always been unique.

Hovering in front of Melania's hourglass, he began to wonder if perhaps, he'd been pulled into another game altogether.

The sand, that had slipped just a few hours ago at a slow, steady pace, swirled in a sluggish wave, forcing the small grains of time to fall quicker into the lower bulb.

His heart froze in his chest. The increased movement could mean only one thing.

Melania's impending death.

He didn't pause to examine his actions or weigh the consequences. He snapped his fingers and the hourglass disappeared from the case and reappeared in his hand. He closed his eyes and envisioned the red thread that bonded Melania to him. Casting his mind out again, he pushed at her psyche and still found her floating in the swirl of darkness.

"Going for a stroll, Daimone?"

He swallowed down a grunt of impatience at the voice that floated up to him from the library floor. Opening his eyes, he glanced down, not surprised to see Moira lounging on a large, winged-back chair and staring up at him with a small smile flirting across her lips.

"I don't have time to play right now, Moira," he said, uncaring if his words came out harsh.

Her soft laughter filled the air. The black, flimsy excuse for a top she wore rode high above her navel as she twisted and swung her pink, leather-clad legs over the arm of the chair, dangling her dark-booted feet over the side and leaning her back onto the other side.

"Everyone has time for me, McDreamy. It's one of the perks of the job." She flicked her long, dark hair over her shoulder and winked at him. "Why don't you float on down here and we'll have a nice chat about that trip you were about to take?"

Before he could respond, her whiskey-brown eyes flashed to mercurial silver.

"I insist."

His fist tightened around the weight in his palm.

Despite his desperate need to get to Melania, even he knew better than to upset Moira, the Keeper of Fate. She knew something. What other reason did she have to interfere?

Jumping down to the ground, he landed lightly on his feet and walked over to her. "What do you know?"

His words lacked any finesse, but he had little time to spare.

She lifted a dark, delicate brow at him. "What? No hello, Moira? How are you doing, Moira?" she said, tsking softly. "Manners, manners."

A low growl rumbled up from his throat as he turned away. He'd never been one for patience.

"Don't you want to know how to save her?"

Moira's taunting words forced his legs to an abrupt stop.

"I repeat," he said, keeping his back to her, "what do you know?"

Her sigh filled the air.

"Fine. You always sucked at playing games, anyway."

He couldn't even scrounge up a smile at the obvious pout in her voice. Silence would get him more answers than questions.

"Your Melania is very special," she said. "Her fate and yours have always been intertwined."

"She's a strong latent."

"She's more than that and you know it. You've always known that."

"Perhaps."

"Ha! Perhaps, he says. Perhaps! Who do you think you're fooling, Daimone?"

Again, he remained silent.

"You know the whole strong, silent type thing is highly overrated."

In a quick flash, she materialized in front of him, her golden skin taut and her eyes rolling with silver.

"You need to tread lightly, Daimone. You can't prevent her death. That's not how it is written."

His lips rose up in a sneer as he raised the hourglass up to her.

"I am *not* the one interfering," he shouted, his words snapping out in a hiss.

He refused to let Melania become a pawn in any petty God games.

Moira's face softened as she reached up and cupped the hourglass in both her palms.

"I know," she said.

A small glow formed where her hands touched the glass. Before he could protest, the orbs disappeared.

A rage stronger than he'd ever felt snapped out of him. In barely a second, he had his fist wrapped around Moira's neck, a roar of anger charging from his throat.

Moira hung in the air, a calmness over her features that only incited him more.

"What have you done?"

She raised a glowing palm up to his eyes. Staring at the hourglass tattooed in the center of her palm, he slowly loosened his clench around her throat, bringing her back down to the ground.

A smile spread across her lips when her feet touched the floor. She placed her glimmering hand over his left arm and hot pain seared across his flesh, smoke slipping from the contact.

She lifted her palm and beneath it he could see the tattoo on his arm now. She'd transferred it to him.

It gleamed softly, the sands in the hourglass still slipping down to the bottom orb.

"I'm evening out the playing field."

He stared at her as comprehension began to dawn.

"I never said interference isn't also fated," she added. "Now go find your little latent It's been a while since someone else besides me caused a ruckus around here."

On a wink, she disappeared in a poof of pink smoke.

A large grin spread across his face. It wasn't often that one literally got a helping hand from destiny.

He strode back to the chair and sat down. Daimone cast out a quick spell, enshrining the hall with protective shields, ensuring there would be no more intruders or disturbances, before he closed his eyes and focused his mind back on Melania.